Leah touched Colt's arm, under the guise of checking out the soft chambray fabric of his shirt

But really it was the rock-hard muscles of the man who was wearing the shirt that impressed her.

Colt sandwiched her hand with his. "That feels nice. Your hand on my arm."

She had to admit it did. More than just nice. Colt was different than she remembered and not just in appearance. Maybe she wasn't the only one who had gone through some hard times and matured these past few years.

"Leah—I just want to be real clear on one point. You're not married anymore, right?"

"That's right."

"Good. I've never kissed a married woman before, and I was hoping this wasn't going to be the exception."

Dear Reader,

If I could wish one thing for you as you read this book it would be that you get swept away. Swept away by Colt Hart, the rodeo cowboy who's been carrying a secret so long that the weight of it is crushing his heart. Swept away by Leah Stockton—a single mom doing her best in trying circumstances, who doesn't need the complication of falling for another cowboy wedded to the road. Or even swept away by Midnight, the stallion the Hart family acquired in a heated bidding war in book one of the series, who may not be worth all the money they paid for him, after all. As the author, I have been enthralled by all of it—the whole world of the Harts of the Rodeo series.

This book was such a pleasure to write, and I want to thank Senior Editor Kathleen Scheibling for creating the Hart family and for setting the story in the most perfect ranching town possible: Roundup, Montana. Thanks also to my editor, Johanna Raisanen, for believing in me and inviting me to contribute to this series. And mega thanks to the other talented authors who also contributed stories. It was so much fun building the world of the Hart family with Cathy McDavid, Roz Denny Fox, Shelley Galloway, Marin Thomas and Linda Warren.

Maybe when you've finished this story you'd like to know more about how I developed the characters for this book. If so, please visit my website—www.cjcarmichael.com—where I'll be posting bonus information about Colt and Leah, as well as contests to win copies from my backlist. You can also keep the dialogue alive by visiting my Facebook page or following me on Twitter. I'd love to hear your feedback about this story.

And finally, don't forget that the Hart family saga continues next month with Roz Denny Fox's *Duke: Deputy Cowboy*.

Happy reading!

C.J. Carmichael

www.cjcarmichael.com

Colton: Rodeo Cowboy

C.J. Carmichael

HARLEQUIN®

entertain, enrich, inspire™

Recycling programs
for this product may
not exist in your area.

ISBN-13: 978-0-373-75417-5

COLTON: RODEO COWBOY

Copyright © 2012 by Carla Daum

ABOUT THE AUTHOR

Hard to imagine a more glamorous life than being an accountant, isn't it? Still, C.J. Carmichael gave up the thrills of income tax forms and double-entry bookkeeping when she sold her first book in 1998. She has now written more than twenty-eight novels for Harlequin Books, and invites you to learn more about her books, see photos of her hiking exploits and enter her surprise contests at www.cjcarmichael.com.

Books by C.J. Carmichael
HARLEQUIN SUPERROMANCE

For Natalie and Caroline with love

Thanks to

The mastermind behind the Hart family series:
Senior Editor Kathleen Scheibling;

My own amazing editor, Johanna Raisanen;

And the creative and talented Cathy McDavid, Roz Denny Fox,
Shelley Galloway, Marin Thomas and Linda Warren.

Chapter One

Clouds were rolling over the hot afternoon sun as an exhausted Colton Hart pulled up to Thunder Ranch in his brand-new Dodge Ram truck with his weathered 22-foot Airstream in tow. A big party was going on at the Hart ranch house this evening, and Colt was late. Not just a few minutes late, but hours. And it wasn't just any party, but a wedding celebration.

His older brother, Ace, had married local ranching girl Flynn McKinley that afternoon. They were madly in love and already expecting a baby. Well on their way to having a perfect life. Something Colt—despite all the rodeo buckles he kept winning—would never have.

He should have cut out early from the rodeo in Central Point and been here. He knew that. The five thousand dollars he'd won simply wasn't worth the price—though he did need that money in his checking account before the first of the month. No running from that cold, hard fact.

Of course the hour delay due to construction on I-90 hadn't helped.

Colt parked the new truck in the lot his mother had given him, about three hundred feet west of the homestead property. He didn't bother unhooking the trailer or reconnecting the water and power. No time.

Inside his trailer, he tossed his dead cell phone on the counter, then added his latest buckle to the collection in his bottom bureau drawer. He'd been gone so much lately the calendar taped to the mirror was still on March. He tore off a couple sheets, then pulled the truck keys from his pocket.

Early that spring he'd won the use of the fully loaded 2012 Dodge Ram for an entire year. He'd never driven, let alone owned, a brand-new vehicle before. The luxury was in danger of becoming addicting. He just might have to buy out the lease at the end of this year—if he could afford to.

He took a few steps to the kitchen, where he ducked his head over the sink and splashed water from a plastic jug over his unshaven face. God, but he'd love a shower. Instead, he made due with a change of clothes, clean Wranglers from his closet and his trademark red chambray shirt.

Colt put on his hat, then stepped out of his trailer into the muggy heat, the heel of his boot sinking into the pine-needle-packed earth. The air was rich with the scent of growing things, tinged with the hickory flavor of his mom's famous barbecue beef. Clouds continued to gather and from the far-off distance, he heard the muffled sound of thunder. It had been a wet spring, now it looked like more rain was coming. Hopefully the storm would hold out a little longer. A path led through the Engelmann spruce toward the main house and he followed the well-trod route, ribs complaining with each breath, muscles everywhere sore and achy.

He lived for the thrill of competing in the rodeo arena, but he had to admit the sport was hell on his body.

The path ended at a fork. Ranch house to the left.

Barns and various other outbuildings to the right. Royce, a long-time ranch hand in his sixties, was sitting at one of the picnic tables that the hired help used for breaks, having a smoke.

"Party going on at the main house," Royce said.

"I know."

"They were expectin' you hours ago."

"I know."

Royce turned his head, took another pull on his cigarette.

Colt waited a second longer. It would only be courteous of Royce to ask how things had gone in Oregon, but Royce didn't say a word. Probably pissed off, like Ace, that Colt wasn't around more to help out at the ranch. But he had financial obligations none of them knew about, and he had to earn extra money somehow.

Colt continued on his way, coming around the back of the house where sparkly lights framed the outdoor pool and the large flagstone sitting area. Outdoor speakers were playing Lady Antebellum's hit song—something about a kiss—while Ace and Flynn fed each other pieces from the wedding cake.

They looked good together. Happy. In love.

Captivated by the sight, Colt watched them for several long moments, before he had to turn away. He felt as if he'd landed facedown in the rodeo arena: throat choked, eyes watering. He couldn't say why their happiness moved him so much. He wasn't one for tears. Or so he'd thought.

He switched his attention to the rest of the family. His mom and Uncle Josh sat at the head table with Josh's sons, Beau and Duke, and Colt's sister, Dinah. Missing was younger brother, Tuf, in limbo after serving in the marines. Wouldn't it have been great if Tuf had somehow shown up for the wedding? No one would have paid Colt much mind if his younger brother had finally returned home.

Colt stepped out of the shadows just as the clouds decided to dump buckets of water onto the scene. No mere shower—this was a deluge. Holding his hat with one hand, shielding his eyes with the other, he dashed with the others toward the open doors that led inside.

He noticed Ace grab Flynn's hand.

"Where are we going?" she gasped.

"To the barn."

Strange choice, Colt thought. But Flynn started laughing and the two of them, so crazy-in-love Colt supposed they were beyond logic, dashed off for the stables. At least this way he wouldn't have to face his brother right away. He knew his excuses for missing the wedding were going to sound mighty lame. Maybe it would be better if Ace didn't have to hear them until after his honeymoon.

He grabbed what remained of the wedding cake from the table and stepped into the house. Next thing Colt knew, he was face-to-face with his mother.

"Well. Look what the storm blew in."

His mom brushed back a strand of her dampened, silver hair. When had the color changed? He couldn't remember, but it had been a long time ago. Worries had come early to Sarah Hart's life. A rancher's life was not an easy one and his father's premature death had placed most of the pressure directly on her shoulders.

Apparently, the stress had been hard on her heart, too. About a month ago she'd had a scare that had sent her to the hospital. Colt had been worried sick then, was still worried now. What would he do—what would any of them do—without their mother in their lives?

The very idea was unthinkable.

He wanted to hug her, and tell her how much she meant to him. But he'd screwed things up. Again. Her expression was as angry as he'd ever seen it.

"You missed your brother's wedding."

He had to look away from her piercing blue gaze. His relationship with Ace was a complicated thing. There was love, sure. But there was also something darker. Something Colt didn't like thinking about, let alone discussing in the open. "He didn't give me much notice."

"Is that the best excuse you can come up with, Colton Adams Hart?"

Colt held his tongue, acutely aware of the others. The family room where they'd all rushed to escape the rain was large, but not so large that everyone couldn't hear their conversation. Dinah grabbed the cake out of his hands, then shook her head as if to say, *You've really done it this time, bro.*

Cousins Duke and Beau were looking desperately in opposite directions, clearly wishing they were anyplace but here. While Uncle Josh seemed sad and disappointed, maybe the hardest reaction of all for Colt to deal with.

Dinah set down the cake then whirled on him. "You missed everything. Ace wanted you for best man, you know."

Colt took a deep breath. No sense telling them about the construction delays. Or the meeting that had run late, but would hopefully lead to a lucrative deal for their new bucking stock program. At this point anything he said would just sound like an excuse.

He glanced at his sister, then back to his mother. "Well, clearly I'm not wanted here. If anything comes up, you can try the Open Range Saloon."

"Colt!" Dinah was incredulous. "You wouldn't dare run out on us now. You just got here."

"Yeah? Watch me." No one called out his name a second time, least of all his mother. Not that he expected anyone to. He'd left too much to chance, given himself no cushion for the unexpected. But contingency planning had never been his strong suit.

LEAH STOCKTON couldn't remember the last time she'd been in a bar alone. Certainly before the kids. Probably before her marriage, too. She looked at her finger, where once she'd worn a thin band of gold embedded with chip diamonds. That finger had been bare for more than a year now.

And *still* her mother refused to accept the divorce.

"I'll have another, Ted." Leah held up her glass to the bartender. He'd owned the Open Range Saloon for as long as she'd been old enough to drink here and he had a disconcerting way of looking at his patrons when he figured they ought to consider slowing down on the alcoholic intake.

Ted was giving her that look now.

"What? This is only my third beer."

"And you weigh all of what—a hundred and ten pounds?"

"It's called being willowy, thank you very much. And it doesn't mean I can't hold my alcohol—though if it eases your conscience, I didn't drive. I'll be walking home."

If she went back.

Silly thought. Of course she'd be going back. Her children were her life now and she was determined to put them first. She just needed a breather for a few hours, that was all. Fortunately they'd already been asleep when she and her mother had their fight. And she'd kept a cool enough head not to slam the door on her way out at the end of it.

Thankfully tomorrow the house she'd rented would be ready for her and the kids to move into. With any luck once they were no longer under the same roof, she and her mom would find it easier to get along.

Ted popped the lid off a bottle of Big Sky and replaced her empty with the full one. She took a long swallow, just daring him to make another comment. But when she glanced at him again, he was looking at someone behind her.

Next thing she knew that someone was setting three darts on the bar next to her glass. The hand holding them was masculine. And his shirt sleeve was red.

A long-ago memory surfaced, of a man who had favored red chambray shirts. Her heart started beating faster—she just couldn't help it. Subtly, she tilted her head so she could check him out.

Tousled sandy hair, nice face, mouth with that adorable, kissable quality that she knew got him into so much trouble. But not with her.

"Well, well, well. Colton Hart. It's been a while."

He touched the brim of his hat. "Indeed it has, Miss Barrel Racing Champion of Roundup High School."

She choked back her smile. Those days seemed so long ago now. "Hardly the highlight of my barrel racing career. I have won a *few* championships since then."

"I know you have. I was there for a couple. Let me see…" He seated himself on the stool next to hers and she couldn't help noticing the breadth of his shoulders, the girth of his biceps. The boy had manned up in the years she'd seen him. And how. Or did she mean *wow*?

Colt didn't seem to notice her checking him out. His

mind was still on rodeos, trying to recall when he'd last seen her. Finally he snapped his fingers. "The Pace Challenge in Omaha back in 2004."

She nodded. "I came in first. And you won best all-around."

He shrugged off his own accomplishment. "You did well at the Snake River Stampede in Nampa, too, as I recall. Was that 2005?"

"Actually, 2006."

"And…that's about the last I remember seeing you." He gave her a steady, serious look. "Rumor had it you met a fellow from Calgary at the Stampede."

She took another long drink of her beer, while he watched thoughtfully.

"But we don't want to talk about that, I'm guessing?"

"You guess correctly."

"So." He tapped the darts he'd placed on the counter. "You game?"

She so was. But strategy dictated she not let him know this. "Why bother? I always beat you."

"Really? Is that how you remember it?" He picked up her half-empty beer and downed the remainder. Then he signaled to the bartender, who'd been listening into their exchange while polishing already-clean glasses. "Ted, we'll need two more of these."

"With a whiskey chaser," Leah added, before Colt escorted her to the dartboard at the back of the bar.

They passed by a table with some people Colt knew, a mixture of guys and women about their age. Leah didn't recognize any faces, but they sure knew Colt.

"Hey, buddy, come and join us," said a dark-haired cowboy, with a nose that had once been very badly broken. "Bring your pretty new friend, too."

Colt waved him off. "Another night, Darcy. Leah and me—we've got business to attend to."

Everyone at the table hooted at that and Leah could feel herself blushing as a result. What was up with that? She was *not* the sort of woman who blushed—was she? But then, it had been a long time since she'd been the focus of this sort of attention. When you normally had a toddler and a preschooler in tow, men tended to keep a polite distance.

The dartboard was at the back of the bar. A throwing line had been etched onto the wooden floor a little less than eight feet away from the board. Colt placed the darts on a nearby table, and they were soon joined by the beer and shooters that they'd ordered.

He took a long drink of the ale then handed her a dart. "Ladies first. Want to play down from 501?"

"Make it 301." Leah removed her light sweater and hung it carefully on the back of her stool. Then she studied the board, trying to decide what strategy to use. In her younger, rodeoing years, she'd spent so much time in bars that she'd been damn near perfect at this game. But now she figured she'd be lucky to hit the bull's-eye. So she took aim, threw…and missed her target by a fraction of an inch. Just enough for the dart to hit a wire and bounce, uselessly, to the floor.

"Out of practice?" Colt asked, his voice all innocent concern.

At a lot of things, Leah thought. Not the least of which was hanging out with an attractive man who was focusing all his attention on her. Not that Colt was hitting on her, or anything. They'd been friends too long for that. But there was a light in his eyes that told her he found her desirable. And that was more than a little distracting for a woman who had spent the past five years mashing baby food and changing diapers.

The kids were past that stage now, thankfully. But looking after them still took the majority of her time.

"So what brings you back to Roundup? Visiting your mom?" Colt took the next dart and went to line up.

He couldn't know how good he looked, standing there. No man wore a pair of Wranglers quite like Colt. How was she supposed to concentrate on their conversation?

Focus, Leah.

"I'm, uh, not visiting. I've moved here. Planning to start my own business."

He'd raised his arm to throw the dart, but went still at her news. "Really?"

"Yes. I've been staying at Mom's for the past few weeks, but tomorrow I move into a house I rented on Timberline Drive."

"Timberline Drive…" A slight frown appeared on his brow. "Is that off Mine Road, near the river?"

"That's it. I got a great deal on the rent. Thankfully it's a lot cheaper to live here than it was in Calgary." She took a drink as Colt turned to the board and threw his dart. Damn thing landed in the outer bull. Clearly Colt wasn't out of practice.

"Nice shot." She tried not to sound grudging.

"By the way, I know it's been a while, but I wanted to tell you I was sorry to hear about your father's passing."

"Thank you." She appreciated Colt's condolences even though more than five years had gone by. The heart attack had been unexpected, but according to the family doctor, at least her father's death had been quick, without time for suffering. After, Leah's mother hadn't had the grit—or the family support—to carry on ranching the way Colt's mother, Sarah Hart, had done after Colt's father's death ten years ago. Prue Stockton had sold their small property within six months, along with the cattle and the few horses they still had around the place—which included Country Girl, Leah's old barrel racing horse.

Leah picked up her second dart. Focusing on the task at hand was what won her prize money when she competed at rodeos. Now she stared at the dartboard with the same intensity, blanking out the bar, the noise, Colt's presence...

To hell with the bull's-eye. She aimed for the sweet spot in the twentieth section, and let out a whoop when her dart landed perfectly in the thin inner portion between the red and green circles.

Colt raised his glass, toasting her success. She joined him at the table, touching her bottle to his, basking in the warmth of his smile. He seemed genuinely glad that she'd done well. Colt wasn't one of those guys who hated losing to a woman. He wasn't a bad loser, period. She'd never seen him so much as throw his hat into the dirt after a bad ride on a bunking bronc.

"Maybe I should concede, after all," he said.

Not at all sure how she would follow up that last, lucky throw, she was quick to agree. "Let's just talk for a while." She took a swallow of beer. "What have you been up to in the last six years?"

"It's been sort of a blur," he admitted. "A lot of time on the road, traveling from rodeo to rodeo."

"Had much success?"

"A little."

She knew what a talented athlete he was in the rodeo arena, yet he wasn't bragging. "Come on. You've finalled in the NFR about eight years straight, haven't you?"

He shrugged. "Yeah, but I still don't have a world championship. Sometimes I wonder if I just don't want it bad enough."

His answer surprised her. The Colt she remembered from high school and the rodeo arena didn't spend a lot of time on introspection. "Rodeo life isn't easy. Maybe you're tired."

He forced a smile. "I can't afford to be. Those purses pay my bills."

"But you work on Thunder Ranch as well, don't you?" And surely his mother paid him a salary for that.

"Not as much as my family would like. But enough about me." He touched the sleeve of her shirt. "I see you still favor purple."

"Lavender," she corrected, pleased that he'd remembered her rodeo colors. She'd packed away the purple cowboy boots and hat, but she still liked to wear her Western shirts.

"It's a good shade for you. Not quite the same color as your eyes. But it makes them stand out, all the same."

Leah had been fed glib lines about her eyes before. Lots of times. But Colt's comment didn't sound superficial. And there was nothing trite about the way he was smiling at her, in a soft and wondering way.

Possibly there were depths to this cowboy that she hadn't appreciated in the past. "And you still favor red." She touched his arm this time, under the guise of checking out the soft, chambray fabric. But really it was the rock-hard muscles of the male who was wearing the shirt that impressed her.

Colt sandwiched her hand with his. "That feels nice. Your hand on my arm."

She had to admit it did. More than just nice. Colt was different than she remembered and not just in appearance. Maybe she wasn't the only one who had gone through some hard times and matured these past few years.

"Leah—I just want to be real clear on one point. You're not married anymore, right?"

"That's right."

"Good. I've never kissed a married woman before and I was hoping this wasn't going to be the exception."

Chapter Two

Colt didn't make a habit of kissing women in public places, either. Generally, he was pretty circumspect when it came to matters of the libido. But this was different. *Leah Stockton* was different. How could you fall in love at first sight with someone you'd known all your life?

But the pretty woman sitting at the bar had caught his eye as soon as he walked into the Open Range Saloon. Her long dark hair and tall, slim body were part of the appeal, but even more was the way she sat on her stool, with saddle-perfect posture, her body relaxed and yet confident and poised for action.

He'd headed straight for her. And then he'd heard her voice as she spoke to the bartender and he'd stopped to listen.

He knew her.

A few seconds later, he had the darts in his hand, ready to issue his challenge. But it wasn't until she looked him in the eyes that it really hit him.

Holy shit, she was a stunner. He'd known Leah since they were kids and yet, somehow, this truth had never sunk in before. Or maybe the passing years had changed her in some subtle, yet earth-shattering way.

Just five minutes into their conversation, it occurred

to him that Leah might be the answer to a question he hadn't been smart enough to ask yet. Being unfocused and aimless in your twenties wasn't such a bad thing. Once you hit thirty, though, your sense of time shifted.

Years went by faster.

You understood that opportunities were either seized, or rarely encountered again.

He wanted to seize. And Leah's eyes told him she was willing. As he leaned toward her, she met him halfway, and when their mouths connected, he stopped thinking, because everything felt so natural and right. This woman made him melt and burn at the same time, and his body felt stirred with a primal, yet mind-blowing intensity.

"We have to leave," he told her.

"Yes."

He left money on the table, next to the drinks they hadn't quite finished. If any of his friends were watching, no one was foolish enough to say anything to him. He felt as if he would have to punch anyone who caused them even a second's delay in getting out of there.

The night air was cool and refreshing after the rain, but it didn't dampen in the slightest his desire to take this woman someplace quiet and private. Leah stumbled slightly as they crossed the street, and he pulled her up closer beside him. Thank God this was Roundup, and there was no traffic, because he couldn't stop himself from kissing her again, right there, in the middle of the street.

Her slender body formed perfectly against his bigger, harder one. He felt her fingers in his hair, her breath on his mouth. He filled his own hands with the curves of her butt, pulling her closer, nuzzling her neck, her collarbone, the silky lobe of her ear.

"Where?" Even his whisper came out sounding hoarse.

"I don't know."

"Can I take you back to my trailer?"

Her lips were against his ear now and he could hear her sigh. "I wish—but no. That won't work."

"Then…?" His mind raced as he tried to think of a suitable place to make love with this beautiful woman. But before he could come up with a solution, she was sighing again.

"You'd better walk me home, Colt. To my mother's place."

Not the answer he'd been hoping for. But maybe, if they were quiet, they could sneak into Leah's bedroom without waking Prue Stockton. Leah was an adult, after all, and he was someone she'd known most of her life.

Leah slipped out of his arms, turned, then stumbled again. "Oops!"

Her giggle was infectious and he had to smile, too, even as he wondered just how much she'd had to drink before he'd shown up at the bar. "Careful, darlin'. Here, let me help you."

He asked for her mother's address, then hand-in-hand they walked the four blocks. He savored each moment with her, his heart full-to-bursting with an emotion he'd never experienced before. He could feel the smile on his face getting bigger each time he looked at her. Even tipsy, Leah had a confident, athletic gait. At the same time she was undeniably female.…

"Here we are." Leah stopped at a Victorian-styled two-story several blocks south of the high school. The house was dark, except for a small exterior lantern to the side of the front door. Two vehicles were parked under the carport to the left of the house—a modest sedan and a Ford truck. The back of the truck was loaded with furniture and boxes.

"The truck yours?"

"You bet."

"Nice." He'd never dated a woman who drove a truck before. Seemed like another good sign to him. He held Leah's hand as they climbed the steps up the porch, then waited as she opened the unlocked front door.

She gave him a smile. "Good night, Colt."

"To hell with that." He pulled her in for another kiss, savoring the softness of her lips, the sweet scent of her hair. Cupping the sides of her face, he pressed the tip of her nose to his. "How about inviting me in, darlin'? I'll make pancakes for your mama in the morning. Win her over with my charm."

This didn't elicit the smile he expected. Instead, Leah frowned. "Those would have to be mighty special pancakes, Colt. My mom doesn't impress easily. Besides, it would be too confusing for Jill and Davey. I haven't dated anyone since I divorced their father."

Suddenly dizzy, Colt put a hand to the wooden railing by the door. "Jill and Davey?"

"My children." Leah looked at him as if he had a screw loose. "You knew about them, right?"

Bloody hell didn't. Colt opened his mouth, not sure what to say. "How old are they?"

"Davey is two, Jill five."

Leah crossed her arms over her chest and narrowed her eyes. Colt knew his reaction was upsetting her, yet he couldn't seem to get his breathing under control or his mind to work properly. He was just so blown away by all of this. How was it that no one—not a family member, or a friend—had mentioned that Leah Stockton had children?

"You're doing the math, aren't you?" Leah finally said. "But I'm not ashamed of the fact that I married Jackson because I was pregnant. It was the right thing to do. As it turned out, we couldn't make the relationship work, but at least I tried."

Oh, God. Stop talking, Leah. He didn't want to hear this. Not any of it.

"You're right. Pancakes were a very bad idea." He took a step away from the door, away from her.

"Colt?"

"I should get going." The chill in the air cut through his shirt and the night sky seemed very bleak all of a sudden.

"You're leaving? Just like that?"

He took another step away. Dinah had said something similar to him, only that afternoon. Badly timed exits were becoming something of a pattern in his life. Colt raised his hat to Leah. In the cold light of day she would be grateful the evening had ended this way.

"I WISH YOU WEREN'T so set on moving out." Prue Stockton, in a pressed housedress with her hair neatly combed, stood at the kitchen counter, dipping homemade bread into her own special egg concoction for French toast.

The sight reminded Leah of Colt's pancake offer of the previous night. An offer he'd backed away from promptly, when he heard about her kids.

Leah took a mug from the counter, filled it with water, which she forced herself to drink, then refilled it with coffee from the carafe on the counter. She didn't begrudge the pain pulsing in her skull—it seemed fair retribution for the mistakes she'd made last night.

Getting tipsy at the Open Range Saloon and picking

up a cowboy was not acceptable behavior for the mother of two small children. She was just thankful that her mother knew none of this.

"I'm thirty-two years old. Don't you think that's too old to be living with my mother?"

"Living with your husband is where you ought to be." Her mom shot her a hard look, then returned her focus to her cooking. "But let's not get into that argument again."

"Let's not," Leah agreed. They had other things to fight about today. Starting with the house she'd rented.

"It won't be easy raising two children on your own. And I have lots of room here."

"I've already signed a one-year lease, Mom, so I'm committed." Leah opened the dishwasher, intending to unload the dinner dishes from yesterday, but her mother had beaten her to it. She decided to set the breakfast table instead.

"Think of the money you could have saved."

Her mother was nothing if not persistent.

"I'm okay for money, Mom. Jackson and I had quite a bit of equity in the house we sold in Calgary." Leah set out the blue-and-white dishes that had been in her family for as long as she could remember. "He's making monthly support payments for the kids, and once I get a few bookkeeping clients, I'll be fine."

"What are you going to do for furniture?"

Leah had brought the kids' beds and all their toys from Calgary. Added to that their clothing and other personal effects, she hadn't had room in the back of her truck for anything else.

She knew her mother had some of the furniture from the old guesthouse on the farm stored in her basement. At one time her grandmother had lived in the small cottage. After she passed on, her mother used the extra room for putting up guests and the occasional farmhand her dad hired during seeding and harvest times.

"I was wondering if I could borrow the bed and sofa from our old guesthouse?"

She half expected her mother to say no. But Prue Stockton wasn't a mean woman. "You may have them, Leah, if you're truly set on moving out. There's a rattan table and four chairs that you're welcome to as well."

"Thanks, Mom. I appreciate that."

Prue sighed. "Better wake the children. Breakfast is just about ready."

Leah headed for the stairs to do as told. Her mother was right about one thing. She did have lots of room in this house. There were four bedrooms and a large bathroom on the upper story. Leah thought it was strange that her mother had moved into such a large place. But maybe a smaller bungalow had been too much of a shock after the sprawling farmhouse Prue had managed for almost thirty years.

Upstairs, Leah peered into the first door on the left, and wasn't surprised to find Jill's bed empty. She found the little girl in her brother's room. She and Davey were sleeping side by side in the single bed, snuggly enclosed by the safety bars that Leah had brought from home.

Leah could never wake her children without first taking a moment to appreciate their sweet little faces in repose. They both had her dark hair and long, thick eyelashes. After a long, cold winter in Calgary, their skin was pale and she looked forward to getting them out for lots of sun and play in their new home. She stroked the side of Jill's face, and her daughter's eyes immediately sprang open.

"Why are you sleeping in here again, honey?"

"Davey had another nightmare."

Leah didn't know why Jill didn't want to own up to the bad dreams. Nor did she understand why Jill chose to go to her brother for comfort, instead of her mom. But she felt it was wise to simply take Jill's answers at face value for now.

"You're a nice sister to take such good care of your brother. Now, why don't you run to the washroom and clean your hands? Grandma's making your favorite breakfast."

"French toast? Yay!" Jill sprang out of the bed, jumping over the safety barrier with the ease of a natural athlete. Given that both her parents had been pros in the rodeo circuit, Leah supposed she shouldn't be surprised.

"Toast?" Davey pushed his head up from the pillow then lifted his butt in the air—a maneuver that looked like a modified child's pose in yoga. "I want fwench toast, Mommy."

Though he was almost three, Davey's speech wasn't very advanced. He spoke in short sentences at best and had trouble with his *r*s. Leah wasn't worried…yet. She figured the divorce and the recent move to Montana might be part of the problem. In time, she hoped Davey would catch up to the verbal ability of his peers.

"Let's go to the bathroom first, honey." He'd only been weaned from his bedtime diaper a few months ago. She'd expected he might regress after the move, but luckily he hadn't.

Five minutes later both children were washed and sitting at the breakfast table. Leah knew her mother would prefer that the children were properly dressed, as well, but she was too much the doting grandmother to insist on it.

As she watched the children tuck in to their food,

Leah couldn't help but think of Colt again. She felt like such a fool for falling all over him last night. She'd actually thought she saw layers of depth in Colt that she'd never seen before. She should have known he wasn't serious, that he was just messing with her.

He'd stopped the charade fast enough when he found out she was a mother. She still wasn't sure what he'd objected to most. The fact that she'd "had" to get married because she was pregnant? Or just the fact that she had kids, and so had responsibilities that he didn't.

At any rate, it was good that he'd revealed his true colors so quickly. Getting involved with a self-absorbed cowboy was one mistake she didn't intend to repeat.

COLT WAS UP BEFORE dawn on Sunday morning, hauling oats and hay into the feeders, ignoring the protests of his rodeo-weary body. Pulled muscles and bruises, sprains and broken bones, came with the territory. Most cowboys worked despite their injuries. He had ridden with bruised ribs, sprained fingers, even a mild concussion, once.

He didn't mind physical pain. On some level he welcomed it.

He'd hardly slept last night after leaving Leah. He'd behaved badly at the end and he knew it. But he'd been so damn disappointed. They could have been good together. If only he'd recognized that years ago, before she married another man—before she had children....

The sun was creeping up on the eastern horizon when one of the ranch hands came out to join him. Darrell was in his mid-forties, a steady family man who had been working at the ranch for as long as Colt could remember. Like Royce, Darrell was a man of few words. Most wranglers were.

"You're out early." Darrell glanced at the feeders. "Looks like you've done my work for me."

Colt removed his leather work gloves and flexed his fingers. "I guess there's more than enough to go around. Or so my brother is always telling me."

"Ace works damn hard," Darrell conceded. "That new stallion isn't helping matters much."

"Midnight?" The black-as-coal recent addition to their breeding stock program was a worry, all right. The family had paid a lot of money at auction for the stallion—the price driven up in a testosterone-fueled bidding war with their neighbor, Earl McKinley.

"Ace has pumped a hell of a lot of time, not just money, into that animal."

"He's been a good breeder out in the field, though, right?"

Darrell nodded. "Yeah, but we need to be able to breed him in a controlled environment. And Midnight still won't stand for that."

Colt nodded thoughtfully. "Think I'll go pay my respects. Maybe give Midnight his workout for the day."

"Good idea. Gracie usually does that, but this is her day off." Darrell gave him a nod, then headed toward the new mares' barn to continue with his chores.

The morning sun was bathing the ranch in gold as Colt made his way to Midnight's stud quarters. Colt was on the road a lot, but usually that only made him appreciate his home all the more when he returned. Late spring was a beautiful time of year with the trees in full leaf, and the grass thick and green. Colt inhaled deeply. Nothing finer than the pure air that blew off the Bull Mountains. He knew he was damn lucky to call Montana home.

If only he could find the inner peace to match his surroundings…

He found Midnight at the far end of his paddock, nuzzling his favorite mare, Fancy Gal. They sure made an odd-looking couple—the pregnant dun mare and the majestic black stallion. Come next spring, it was going to be interesting to see what their foal looked like.

Colt climbed over the fence and paused to see how Midnight would react. The stallion shook his mane and pranced backward a few steps. Colt had to admit that all of Ace's doctoring was paying off. The stallion's coat was glossy and thick, and he'd lost that wild look that spoke of the abuse he'd suffered at the hands of the damned foreman who'd been hired by Midnight's previous owners.

"Hey, boy. How's it going?" Colt moved slowly toward the horse. He supposed Midnight was on break from his stud duties while Ace was on his honeymoon. "Feel like stretching out those long legs of yours today?"

Midnight jerked his head upright as Colt approached, and laid his ears back.

"It's okay, boy. No one's going to hurt you here on Thunder Ranch. You've figured that out by now, haven't you?" From the pocket of his denim jacket, he pulled out one of Angie Barrington's special horse cookies. Along with carrots they were Midnight's favorite treat.

Cautiously Midnight accepted the goody, then backed right off again.

"You miss Gracie, don't you, boy? Well, don't worry. I'm not going to hurt you." He kept talking as he moved closer, angling the horse toward the gate that led to the dirt-packed, round arena they used for exercising and training young horses.

Midnight was no fool. He knew where Colt wanted·

him to go. Yet he resisted. Why? Colt wondered. He studied the horse's dark eyes, trying to understand what was going on in his head.

Eventually Colt coaxed the stallion into the arena where he used hand gestures and encouraging words to get Midnight to run laps around the perimeter of the fence. A few times Midnight seemed to get into it, but then he would fall back and give Colt a resigned look as if to say, *This is it? This is the most excitement you can give me?*

"Not too enthusiastic, is he?"

Colt started at the sound of his mother's voice. He turned around and saw her leaning against the fence, one booted foot on the lower rung. She was wearing an old corduroy coat she'd owned for ages and her cheeks were ruddy from the cool morning air.

"Sorry about yesterday, Mom."

"It's Ace and Flynn you need to apologize to."

"I will. As soon as they're back from their honeymoon." He glanced back at Midnight, who had stopped running and was nibbling at the grass growing at the edge of the fence. "Has anyone tried riding him yet?"

His mother looked amused. "That horse was born to buck. I don't think anyone would dare."

"Well, maybe we should let him compete in rodeos again. He needs to get some exercise somehow. Loping around this arena just doesn't cut it."

"That would be pretty risky, don't you think? What if he was injured?"

"You have a point," Colt conceded. "Okay, boy." He opened the gate to the pasture. "That's enough for today."

Midnight didn't need to be invited twice. He trotted quickly out of the arena and rejoined his mare.

"By the way, son, was that a new truck I saw parked by your trailer?"

"Yeah. I won the use of it this spring, but only picked it up on my way to Oregon. It handles like a dream. I'm thinking of buying out the lease when the year is up."

His mother said nothing to that. She never asked him what he did with his rodeo winnings and he never offered any information. But however you looked at it, the new truck was a luxury. One he could hardly afford. But he was thirty-two years old and lived in a trailer that was almost as old as he was.

And that new truck was so damn sweet...

"You'll join Dinah and me for breakfast?" She dug her hands into the pockets of her jacket as she gave him a sideways glance. "And then to church, after?"

"Sorry, Mom. There's something else I need to do." Leah was on his mind. He'd behaved badly yesterday. No changing the past. But there was one thing he could do today to prove that he wasn't a total jerk.

Chapter Three

Leah spent the morning cleaning her new house. Her mother alternated between helping and playing with the kids in their new backyard. With the river so close by, Leah wouldn't have rented the place if it hadn't been securely fenced. As a bonus, the yard had a built-in sandbox and swing set and a paved patio that was perfect for Davey to ride his plastic tractor on.

"The kitchen is sparkling," Prue commented, as she grabbed a couple of juice boxes out of the fridge for the children. Earlier she'd helped Jill change into a pair of shorts and a T-shirt that matched. She was trying to wean her granddaughter from her penchant for wildly colorful, mismatched outfits. Leah wished her luck with that one.

"Thanks, Mom. It does look good, doesn't it?"

"Have you tackled the basement yet?"

Leah wrinkled her nose. "No. It's too big of a project. We'll just use the main floor for now." It would be squishy, though, as she'd hoped to put a playroom for the kids, as well as her office, down there. But both she and her mother had noticed a foul odor this morning when they checked the place over.

"Smells like mildew," her mother had said. "I wish

you'd told me you were thinking of renting this place. Houses this close to the river are prone to flooding."

Oh, great. Just what she needed to hear. Now Leah knew why the rent had been such a great deal. At some point she would have to talk to her landlord about ripping out the carpet and scrubbing and repainting the walls. But until then the kids could share a room, and she'd use the main-floor bedroom for her office. All the toys were just going to have to go in the living room.

They'd get by.

Leah tossed the rag she'd used to wash the floor into a pail by the door. "I think we're ready to move in now. I'll unload the boxes from the truck if you don't mind staying with the kids."

"Actually, I think I should take them back to my place. Davey's rubbing his eyes and there's no place to put him down for his nap."

She gave her mom a hug. "That would be perfect, thanks. We'll have to transfer their booster seats into your car."

"I can do that. You just keep on with what you're doing."

Prue made a game of it, telling Jill and Davey it was time to board the train back to grandma's house. "Choo! Choo!" Davey called, as she buckled him into the backseat. Leah waved until they'd driven out of sight, a smile on her face. It was at moments like this that she knew she'd done the right thing in moving back to Roundup. Her mother was an awesome grandma.

And now she was free to get her work done.

Leah opened the tailgate to her truck, then reached for the closest box. Within an hour she had unloaded everything—even the kids' beds and bureaus, which weren't very heavy. Only the furniture in her mother's basement remained. But that would have to wait until tomorrow. The fellow she'd hired to help her didn't work on Sundays.

She was closing the tailgate when a black Dodge Ram pulled up across the street. She brushed her hands against her jeans and shook her head as Colt stepped out of the driver's seat.

"You've got to be kidding."

"Just wondering if I could give you a hand?"

Gone was the sexy, flirty voice he'd used on her at the bar. Today he looked serious. Maybe even a little sheepish. He was in jeans and a clean work shirt. No red chambray today, thank goodness. He held his hat in his hands, his stance that of a little boy feeling guilty about something.

As he damn well should.

She wanted to tell him to go to hell. But after last night, he owed her. Besides, she had some business to discuss with Colt. Something she should have brought up yesterday if she hadn't been having too much fun.

"That depends on how much time you've got."

"As much as you need."

Oh, she highly doubted that was true.

"There's a bed, a sofa and a table-and-chair set back in Mom's basement and I can't move them myself...."

"I'd be glad to help. Let's take my truck. It's bigger."

For the first time she noticed his vehicle. It was a newer model, with all the extras. "Sweet. Can I drive?"

She could have sworn his face grew paler. But he handed her the keys with only the slightest of hesitations, then opened the driver's side door for her. When she was settled, he loped around the truck and slid into the seat next to her.

She was aware of his eyes on her as she made the

necessary adjustments to the seat and the mirrors. Only when she was done did he ask, "So…how's the head this morning?"

When she grimaced, he chuckled. "Thought so."

"What's that supposed to mean?"

"You had a few too many. That's all."

She groaned. "Was it that obvious?"

He reached for her hair and gave a little tug. Just a playful gesture…so why did her heart do a little flip?

"Let's just say you were a little unsteady on your feet. Also, let's face it—if you hadn't had a few beers, no way would you have let me kiss you."

She turned her eyes briefly from the road to check his expression. Really? Was that the way he wanted to play this? Well, fine with her. "So true," she said coolly. "But even single mothers need to have a little fun now and then."

"I suppose that's true," he said, his voice suddenly tight.

"I wouldn't want our foolishness last night to affect our friendship, Colt."

"Foolishness?"

"Good," she said, ignoring the question in his voice. "Glad we see it the same way." She turned the corner to her mother's block, then pulled up into the driveway. "Here we are. Hope you're ready to work."

LEAH HAD BRUSHED OFF their evening together as "foolishness." Colt knew he should feel glad. He was off the hook and back in the sea—free and unencumbered, as always.

Maybe the gladness would come later, when the good news had a chance to sink in.

For now, he was satisfied to put his muscles to good

use. The move didn't take long. At one point Prue Stockton stepped out on the porch to watch for a few moments. Then she gave him a polite nod and went back inside with the kids.

As for Jill and Davey, he didn't see any sign of them at all. Which he was grateful for. He had no experience with kids and had no idea what to do or say around them.

Within two hours all the work was done. Leah's new house was okay, Colt thought. Kind of small, especially the kids' bedroom. They'd barely managed to fit in the two beds, and had been forced to stuff the bureau into the small closet.

That stench coming from the basement wasn't good, either. But Leah told him she was planning to talk to her landlord about tearing out the old carpet and painting the walls. Maybe he'd offer to help.

That was the sort of thing a friend would do, after all.

Friend. His mind grated over the word every time he thought of it in conjunction with Leah. Because she was just as attractive to him now as she'd been last night at the Open Range.

Get over it, he told himself. She'd offered him an olive branch this morning and he should be damn grateful she'd given him that much.

They were in the living room now. Leah had her hands on the slim curves of her hips. "Hmm. I'm thinking the sofa would look better on that wall." She pointed to the one opposite the window. "What do you think?"

He had a mother and a sister, so knew better than to offer an opinion. "Whatever you say." Obediently, he picked up one end of the sofa and maneuvered it into place.

Leah smiled. "That is better, thanks." She glanced

around the room, then sighed. "I think we're finally done."

He had to get her out of there before she thought up another redecorating idea. "I don't know about you, but I'm hungry. Want to grab a late lunch at the Number 1? Sierra serves a mean roast beef special on Sundays."

Leah considered the offer. "Let me phone my mother first and see how the kids are doing."

He waited while she pulled her cell phone from her pocket. Like him, she had an iPhone, only instead of a horse she used a picture of her two kids for her wallpaper. After a brief conversation she gave him the nod. "Mom said we should go ahead. They had their lunch an hour ago. But where is the Number 1—is it new? I don't remember a café by that name. A coal mine, yes, but not a café."

Colt waited while she locked up her new home, then led her to the passenger side of his truck. His day was looking up now that he'd convinced her to have lunch with him and he was happy to bring her up to speed on some of the happenings she'd missed when she lived in Calgary.

"Sierra Byrne owns and runs the Number 1. She named the café in honor of her grandfather, a miner who drowned when the Number 1 was flooded back in… I don't know when exactly. A long time ago. It's been open about four years."

"Did Sierra grow up here?"

Relieved that Leah didn't ask to drive again, Colt walked around to the driver's side and pressed the buttons to return his seat and mirrors to their original positions. His new truck had impressed her. It was kind of ridiculous how happy that made him.

"Nah, Sierra's parents lived in Chicago. But her mother

and Aunt Jordan grew up in Roundup and Sierra's family spent summers at their cabin along the Musselshell River."

Leah glanced out the window as they drove along Highway 87 toward First Street. "Must have been some change moving from Chicago to here."

Her comment made Colt wonder how Leah herself was making the adjustment. "You miss Calgary?"

She was quiet for a bit, then shifted her gaze from the town to him. "If the past six years taught me anything, it's that I'm a small-town girl at heart."

There was a world of unhappiness in that comment, Colt thought. He parked across the street from the red-brick building that housed the Number 1.

"Hey, isn't this the old newspaper building?" Leah whistled. "Sierra sure fixed it up nicely."

"Wait until you taste the food." Colt was about to open his door when Leah stopped him with a hand on his shoulder.

"Hang on a sec. You're still not off the hook where last night is concerned."

"I'm not?"

"Like I told you before, I'm planning to start a new business here in Roundup. I've got a business diploma with an agricultural accounting concentration and—" she took a deep breath "—I was hoping Thunder Ranch might be my first client."

It took him a few seconds to process what she was saying. "Seriously? You want to be an accountant?"

"It's a good job for a working mother. Tell me—who does your family's books now?"

"My mother."

"Do you think she'd consider hiring outside help?"

He thought about the health scare she'd had recently,

and all the extra work that had fallen on her and Ace's shoulders since they added the bucking horse breeding program. Most everyone in his family would rather be working on the land and with the animals than doing paperwork in the office. "I'll talk to her about it—okay?"

"That would be great."

He adjusted his hat, then gave her a cautious glance. "So we're square now?"

"What do you think?"

Colt laughed. She kept him hopping, that was for sure. And if he had to be on the hook with someone, Leah Stockton would be his first pick.

THE INSIDE OF the café had been decorated in keeping with the mining theme, with historical photographs on the walls and a shelf full of mining artifacts. Leah especially liked the dramatic color scheme—sparkly red tables and black leather seats. Colt led her to a corner booth, and she was charmed to see a miniature coal bucket in the middle of the table holding the condiments.

Colt waved at someone out of her line of sight. She turned to see a curvy woman, about her age, in a red apron delivering two plates of the lunch special to the table behind them. When she was done, she gave Colt a warm smile.

"Hey, Sierra. How're you doing?"

"Business is good, so I'm happy. I'll take your order in a sec, Colt. Just let me get you some water, first."

She turned on her heel, heading for the kitchen, and Leah cleared her throat.

"Um…either I'm invisible, or that woman only has eyes for you. She didn't even glance at me."

Colt flashed a smile—the kind he'd used a lot the previous evening. "Darlin', don't tell me you're jealous."

"Right. After last night? I don't think so."

Sierra returned then, and Leah flashed a smug look at Colt when she had only one glass of water. *See—I was right. She didn't even notice me!*

"Oh, dear." Sierra looked flustered. "I'm sorry, I didn't realize you had a guest."

Colt made the introductions, then asked for the lunch special.

"I'll have the same, please." Leah had to admit that Sierra was making up for her earlier rudeness by being especially attentive now. She quickly brought an extra glass of water to the table, and apologized again for her oversight.

When they were alone once more, Colt's expression turned serious. "About last night—I want to apologize."

"Really, for which part? For hitting on me like I was one of your buckle bunnies? Or running for the hills once you found out I had children?"

He grimaced. "When you put it that way…"

"Maybe you were judging me because you figured out Jackson and I got married because I was pregnant?"

Colt looked truly miserable now. "God, no, I wasn't judging you. I'm the last—" He turned his head away and drummed his fingers on the table as he searched for the right words to say. "My Uncle Josh likes to say that if you want to be successful in life, figure out what you're not good at, and don't do it."

Leah had to smile. That sounded like something her father might have said.

"And what I'm not good at is kids. And responsibility. I'm not like Ace, or my father, or my uncle—I don't know why. I just was born with…something missing."

Did he really believe this crap? No one knew better than Leah that people weren't born with the ability to be responsible parents. She certainly hadn't been mentally prepared to be a mother when Jill was born. She'd loved barrel racing and she'd enjoyed the travel and meeting new people. Settling down hadn't been in her plans, at all.

But now that she had Jill and Davey, she was grateful for how her life had worked out. She had a feeling that Colt wouldn't understand, even if she tried to explain. Best to keep things simple between them.

"I get it. You don't want to be involved with a woman who has children. And you're probably right. We were always best at being just friends."

"Right." Colt didn't sound convinced, however. The look he gave her was rather pensive, in fact.

Sierra arrived with their food then, and she set the fragrant plates in front of them. "Hope you enjoy. Let me know if you need anything else."

For a few minutes Leah and Colt ate in silence, though Leah couldn't remember when she'd last had such a small appetite. Then Colt put down his fork.

"Everything you just said makes perfect sense. But you have to admit…we did have something there for a bit, didn't we?"

Leah didn't dare reply, or look up from her food, because she'd been thinking the exact same thing.

Chapter Four

After lunch Colt dropped Leah back at her place. He watched her walk away from him, her long dark hair swaying from side to side with each stride. She gave him a final wave before getting in her truck to drive back to her mother's.

He ought to be pleased with how the day had gone. He'd made his apologies and atoned for his rude behavior by helping Leah move into her new home. They'd cleared the air between them, and agreed that they were better off staying just friends.

But he didn't *feel* pleased. He felt...restless and a little, well, unhappy. The feeling wasn't a new one. But it was becoming more pervasive. Used to be he'd have a couple of good weeks, maybe even a month, when he'd be happy to be back home after a series of rodeos. Now it didn't seem to matter where he was...he was always wishing he could be somewhere different.

Colt drove back downtown to the post office. He parked, then reached for the stamped envelope he'd put in the glove box earlier. He could have set up automatic payments with his bank, but he got some satisfaction out of this monthly ritual. He went to the drop box on the wall of the post office, hesitating for a moment, then releasing the letter into the capable hands of the U.S. postal system.

He liked knowing that in a couple of days the letter, with his handwriting, would be sitting on their kitchen counter. Tangible evidence of his existence.

Colt returned to his truck and headed back to the ranch. He wished he could feel enthusiastic about something. *Anything.* Spending time with his family, working with the horses, checking in with Uncle Josh on the cattle side of their operation. But he didn't.

The source of the problem went back twelve years. His father had still been alive then, and Colt had considered going to the old man for advice. But the timing had been bad. Ace had just been accepted into veterinary college and their parents had been so pleased. So Colt had kept everything to himself, and done what had seemed to him to be the right thing at the time.

Only ever since then, and especially in the last few years, he'd started to wonder if he'd been wrong. Dead wrong.

Last night Leah had said something to him about being proud of her decision, of knowing she'd done the right thing.

And that was the crux of his problem, Colt realized. He wasn't proud. In fact, he was damned ashamed.

THE DAY HAD TURNED unseasonably hot, almost eighty degrees Colt figured, as he strode across the pasture looking for Midnight. He could feel the prickle of sweat under his hat, and thought longingly of a swim in the family's pool.

But first he needed to talk to his mother. She hadn't been in the house, so the office in the barn was his next guess. He figured he'd say hello to Midnight on his way.

The stallion and Fancy Gal were grazing laconically in the shade of an aspen grove. As soon as Midnight spotted him, he snorted and tossed his head. Almost as if he were trying to say hello.

"You are one fine-looking animal," Colt said as he drew closer. "And no, Fancy Gal, I am not speaking about you." He gave the mare a friendly scratch on the side of her neck and when she nuzzled up to his shoulder, he laughed.

"You know what I have, don't you?" He pulled the AB Horse Treat out of his shirt pocket and broke her off a piece. The rest he offered to Midnight.

The stallion was more stand-offish than the mare. He thrust his head back and glared at Colt with his dark brown eyes, before condescending to take the food.

Once he had the cookie, though, Midnight backed off. He munched through the treat in no time, then gave Colt another look. This time Colt felt as if the animal were pleading with him. And not for another cookie.

"What do you want, Midnight Express?" Colt didn't think he was projecting his own emotions on the animal, when he sensed a certain restless longing in him. Maybe he should find out more about Midnight's history and see if there were clues to why he wasn't settling in more easily.

Colt left the horses, then made his way to the equestrian barn. "Mom, you here?"

"In the office, Colt."

He found her behind the large oak desk, glasses settled halfway down her nose, frowning at the adding machine. "Darn thing just keeps making mistakes today."

Colt noticed several of the filing cabinet doors were open. Some of the papers had spilled onto the scarred plank floor. He bent over to pick them up. "What's this? Some kind of cash-flow statement?"

"It's a condition of our bank loan. We're supposed to send them these reports every quarter. This one is due at the end of the month."

Colt couldn't have asked for a better lead-in. "Well, interesting you should say that, Mom, because I was just talking to someone who's setting up a new bookkeeping business in Roundup and she's looking for clients."

His mother peered at him over the top of her glasses. "Go on."

"The… Well, the woman is Leah Stockton. Do you remember her?"

"Sure do. She and Cheyenne Sundell were the competitors to beat back in Dinah's barrel racing days. She used to ride that beautiful paint."

"Country Girl," Colt recalled. Leah's horse had not only been a beauty, but she'd also been light on her feet, too. He'd never seen a horse make tighter turns around a barrel.

He moved toward the whiteboard on the wall where they kept track of the rodeo bookings for the bucking stock. "Looks like a busy schedule."

"Sometimes I wonder if it isn't too busy. If our breeding program is as successful as Ace thinks it could be, maybe we could afford to slow up a little next year."

"In the meantime, it seems like a smart idea to get you some office help. You know, Leah doesn't barrel race anymore. She has two little kids to support."

"I did hear about that. She married some cowboy she met at the Calgary Stampede, but they ended up divorced. Her mother is pretty upset about it."

"Well, that's life. Bad things happen."

"Unfortunately that's true." His mother glanced at

the papers scattered over her desk, then frowned again at the adding machine. "Does Leah have any experience doing books for a ranch?"

"I'm not sure. But she does have an accounting diploma so she must know something."

"I suppose I could give her a chance. Lord knows I'd be happy to spend less time in here." She glanced at the far wall, where a couple of shelves held some of her children's and even a few of her husband's rodeo trophies. "Give her a call and see if she can make it here for Monday morning."

LEAH EXPECTED settling the kids to sleep that evening in their new bedroom would take longer than usual. She'd done her best to make the small room feel like home. They'd unpacked toys together and she'd hung many of the pictures from their old rooms in Calgary, including several of their dad. The twin beds were made up with Davey's Thomas-the-Train and Jill's Dora-the-Explorer comforters.

They'd already had showers and brushed their teeth in the new bathroom. Now Leah asked them to put their dirty clothes in the hamper, then climb into their beds. As they scampered around the room collecting socks and underwear, her phone chimed.

She pulled it out of her back pocket and saw a text from Colt.

Mom wants to meet with you about the job. Tomorrow good?

Leah smiled, then slipped the phone back into her pocket. "Who wants to read *Melanie Mouse's Moving Day?*"

"I do!" Jill went to the large wicker basket where they'd unpacked their books and pulled out the well-worn picture book.

"Me, too." Davey scrambled up beside his sister, leaving room in the middle for Leah. She accepted the book from Jill, glad she'd had the foresight to buy a hardcover, since they'd been reading this story a lot lately. Neither one of the kids seemed to get tired of it. Usually at the end came lots of questions, which Leah patiently answered, over and over. Her children had been through many changes with the divorce and the move and she wanted them talking to her about their feelings, not bottling them up inside.

Today, though, Jill had a new question for Leah.

"Why couldn't we stay at Grandma's house, Mommy? She wants us to."

"Well, when I was a little girl, like you, I lived with your grandmother, because she was my mom. But I'm an adult now. And once you're an adult, you're too old to keep living with your parents."

"I won't ever be too old to live with you," Jill said.

"Me, too," Davey said, giving her a fierce hug.

"You can stay as long as you want," Leah promised.

"But if we left, would you cry like Grandma does?" Jill asked.

This was news to Leah. "Did you see your grandmother cry?"

Jill nodded. Davey leaned in close and whispered. "She was sad."

"Really?" Leah swallowed, feeling some tears of her own welling up. "We'll have to give Grandma lots of hugs and kisses the next time we see her so she'll be happy again. Just like this—" Leah put an arm around each of her children and took turns kissing one, then the other. Soon, they were tumbling on the bed and giggling.

Which wasn't exactly calming them down for sleep.

But she didn't want them going to bed sad, either.

She decided to read them another book, a silly, fun book by Dr. Seuss, and then finished with the classic *Goodnight Moon,* which the children read to *her* since they knew it by heart.

"I love you, peanuts. Sleep well." She gave them final kisses, pulled up their covers, then left the room, door open, night-light glowing.

She would have liked a little time to relax with a cup of tea and the latest episode of *The Good Wife,* but she still had her own bed to make and clothing to unpack. She was crossing the hall when her iPhone rang. She answered quickly, not wanting the chime from *Modern Family* to wake the kids.

"Hello, Mom." She fought to keep her tone friendly, even though she was upset at her for crying in front of the kids. Her mom had been a big help since she'd moved back to Roundup. And she did appreciate that. But her children needed less drama in their lives. Not more.

"I didn't get a chance to tell you this earlier, Leah, but Jackson called the house today."

"Really?" She hadn't heard from her ex in over a week.

"He wants you to phone him back."

"Did he talk to the kids?" They hadn't mentioned anything, so Leah would be surprised if he had.

"No. They were napping, so I never thought to mention it."

It shouldn't have been up to her mother. Jackson should have asked.

"Leah, you will call him back?"

"Yes. I'll dial him on Skype tomorrow morning so the kids can talk to him, too."

"Maybe it would be better to call him tonight while they're sleeping. So the two of you can have a private chat."

"Mom, there is nothing private to be said. The divorce is final. Our only connection now is our children."

There was a long silence. Then her mother said, "This wouldn't have anything to do with Colton Hart helping you with the move today, would it?"

"Mom, no! I haven't seen him in years. We just happened to run into one another at the Open Range last night."

"Is that where you stormed out to? I thought I could smell stale beer on your clothes when I put them in the washer."

Oh, my Lord. *Give me patience.* Her mother was making her feel like an adolescent again.

"Yes, Mom, I went to the bar for a few drinks last night." Leah opened the black garbage bag that held her bedding and pulled out her sheets. She pressed the speakerphone option, then set the phone on her nightstand so she could start making up her bed. "I am thirty-two, remember? And since I know you're about to ask—no, there is nothing romantic going on with Colt and me."

Not anymore, there wasn't.

"I'm relieved to hear that. The Harts are a good family, but everyone knows Colt is the black sheep."

Really, Mom? Black sheep? Leah bit back a sarcastic comment, knowing there was no point in starting an argument she couldn't win.

"The real reason I was talking to Colt was because

I wanted him to ask his mother about me doing some bookkeeping for Thunder Ranch." Her mother knew about her plans to run her own home business. She'd shocked Leah by actually being supportive.

"That's a good idea."

"Thank you. I just received a message that Sarah Hart wants to interview me tomorrow. Is there any chance you could watch the kids for me, again?"

"I have coffee plans with some friends in the afternoon, but my morning is free. I'd be happy to have them for a few hours. Would that be enough time?"

"Lots. Thanks so much, Mom. I'll bring them over around nine-thirty."

Leah sat on her bed and picked up her phone to end the call with her mother then typed a reply to Colt's message. Great! Tomorrow at ten, okay?

His reply came a few seconds later.

That works. Now you owe me, darlin.

Chapter Five

Efforts to reach Jackson on Skype the next morning were not successful. Leah ended up leaving him an email message, asking when the best time to talk to him would be. *The kids miss you,* she added, hoping that would provide incentive for him to answer promptly.

Putting her ex-husband out of her mind, Leah connected her computer, then checked the directions to Thunder Ranch. When she was sure she knew where she was going, she loaded the kids into the truck and drove to her mother's.

As soon as she saw her mother's face, however, she could see that she wasn't well. "Do you have a migraine coming on, Mom?"

"I'm afraid so."

Leah kept a hold on Davey and Jill, who had been about to run to their grandmother to give her the hugs and kisses they'd talked about yesterday. "Hang on, guys. Grandma's head is hurting today. Don't touch her, okay? And try to be very quiet."

She took a closer look at her mom. "Have you taken your pain meds?"

"Yes."

"And have you eaten anything today?"

"Toast and coffee."

"That's good. Why don't you lie down in your room, and I'll bring you some water." She went to the kitchen, took out a glass and filled it with ice-cold water from the tap.

"I'm so sorry about this, Leah. I know you have that appointment at Thunder Ranch. Maybe if you turn the TV to some children's programming, the kids and I will make out okay until you return."

"No way, Mom." She felt guilty enough already about how much her mother had been helping her. Maybe she was pushing it and that was why she'd come down with the headache today. She didn't get them often, but when she did, they were dreadful.

"But your meeting..."

"I'll figure something out. I'm more worried about you right now." She took her mother's arm and led her to the bedroom. She helped her settle and left the glass of water on the nightstand. "Will you be okay for a few hours?"

"Oh, yes."

"Good. I'll come by around lunchtime. For now, please get some rest."

"Thank you, Leah." Her mother's eyes were already fluttering closed.

Leah found the children in the living room. Jill had the remote pointed at the TV and was changing channels while Davey kept saying "no" to everything she found.

"Jill, please hand me that." Leah switched off the television. "We have to get back into the truck. Since Grandma's sick we're switching to Plan B."

"What's Plan B, Mommy?" Jill asked.

She had no idea.

WITH THE KIDS STRAPPED into the truck, Leah dialed the number for Thunder Ranch. Sarah Hart answered.

"Hi, Mrs. Hart, this is Leah Stockton. I'm afraid I have a babysitting issue this morning. Could we please reschedule our meeting for tomorrow?" She hated asking, feeling as if this could only hurt her chances for landing the job.

But Sarah proved understanding. More than Leah could have expected. "No need for that. Bring them with you. And don't forget their swimsuits."

"Are you sure?"

"You bet. It's been too many years since we've had young ones around here."

"Gosh, well thanks, Mrs. Hart. See you at ten o'clock, then."

"Looking forward to it, Leah."

After disconnecting the call, Leah turned to the children. "Anyone want to go to a ranch?"

"Yes!" Davey clapped his hands, then asked, "What's a wanch?"

"It's a place with cows and horses," Jill said authoritatively. "Right, Mom?"

"Yes. And they have a swimming pool, too."

"Awesome." Jill's violet-blue eyes went round with wonder.

Leah drove back to the house on Timberline Drive and stuffed a backpack with books, snacks and sunscreen as well as the kids' bathing suits and towels.

For all the years she'd known Colt, Leah had never been to Thunder Ranch, which was on the opposite side of Roundup from the farm where she'd been raised. The first ten miles were along Highway 12, but when she turned south off that, she lowered her speed and opened the windows so they could enjoy the scent of growing hay and the tang of the ponderosa pines.

The light blue sky was clear of clouds and provided the perfect backdrop to the gentle hills of sage-colored grass, low-growing ponderosa pine and sandstone rock outcroppings. Every breath smelled like home to Leah, who hadn't appreciated, until this moment, just how much she missed her own family's farm.

At last she arrived at the mile-long driveway that led to Thunder Ranch. Taller spruce trees grew on either side of the well-maintained gravel road until finally Leah could see the main house. Large, but not pretentious, with wood siding and a fieldstone wall, the home blended into the surroundings with an air of permanent belonging.

Again, Leah couldn't help but think of the farmhouse where she'd spent her childhood. She understood why her mother had to sell after her father's death. But she wondered if any house would ever truly feel like home to her, the way that one had.

The new house in the suburbs of Calgary where she'd lived with Jackson certainly hadn't. Nor, she had to admit, did the place she'd just rented on Timberline Drive. She looked back at her children. What did home mean to them? she wondered. She'd moved them around so much the past few months....

"Is this the ranch?" Jill asked, doubtfully. "Where are the horses?"

"This is just the house. See those buildings down there? Those are the barns where the horses live. But I bet most of the horses are outside today. On ranches the horses live in fenced areas that are called pastures."

Leah hoped she would have a chance to show them the livestock later. But for now, she helped them out of the truck, then grabbed her briefcase and their back-pack. Before they had reached the big front door, Sarah had it opened.

The matriarch of the Hart family was in jeans and a neatly pressed gingham blouse. She was also wearing a beautifully tooled leather belt, which had to have been crafted by Sarah's nephew Beau Adams. Leah had admired his leather goods at the Western Wear and Tack Shop in town.

"Hi, Mrs. Hart. These are my children, Jill and Davey."

Her son stuck his chest out proudly. "I'm Davey."

"Thanks for clearing that up for me, Davey." She winked at Leah. "So you must be Jill."

Leah's daughter smiled, and Leah wondered what Sarah thought of Jill's bright pink leggings and green-and-orange striped T-shirt. The combination made Leah want to reach for her sunglasses, but Sarah made no comment.

"We might as well go straight to the equestrian barn since that's where the office is."

And Colt? Leah had thought about the possibility of seeing him today when she'd dressed in her favorite lavender shirt. She'd even stared in the mirror, remembering the comment he'd made about purple bringing out the color of her eyes. But they'd looked the same to her. Just cowboy flattery on Colt's part. She had to remember to watch out for that.

Sarah Hart offered her hands to the children, and Leah was relieved when they each took one as if it were the most natural thing in the world. They weren't usually shy, her children, but it would have been just her luck if they'd decided to be so today.

"Can we see a cow, Mrs. Hart?" Davey asked.

"And ride a horse?" Jill added.

"I'm afraid the cattle are grazing in the south pasture this time of the year. But we have some new foals that are awfully cute. As for riding a horse, Jill, maybe one day. How about going for a swim, instead?"

She had been riding horses at Jill's age, Leah reflected. But she was glad Sarah hadn't encouraged the idea. If Jill got the bug, she knew only too well what would come next. And providing horse lessons wasn't something she was financially equipped to do just yet. Once she had some clients lined up, that would be a different matter. Landing Thunder Ranch was key to all of that. With Sarah Hart's stamp of approval, she'd be home free.

As they neared the equestrian barn, Davey wrinkled his nose. "What's that smell?"

A ranch hand in her forties happened to be coming out of the barn at that moment. She laughed and answered easily, "That's the smell of money in Montana, young man."

"It certainly is," Sarah agreed with a smile. "Hi, Gracie. This is Leah Stockton and her children, Jill and Davey. Leah's here to look at the books. She may soon become our new accountant."

"Well, why don't I show these young ones some of our new foals while you and Leah talk numbers?"

"Thank you, great idea. We should only be fifteen minutes or so. This way, Leah." Sarah led her past some empty stalls to a room about fifteen feet by twelve on the right side of the barn. Here was a desk, two worn leather chairs, a filing cabinet and plenty of shelves, most of which were filled with rodeo trophies and framed photographs of the family and their prized livestock. Propped up against the wall, apparently waiting to be hung, was a large picture of a magnificent black stallion.

"Wow, he's a beauty."

"That's The Midnight Express, our newest acquisition." Sarah sighed. "He sure is a gorgeous-looking animal, but he's proving to be a bit of a handful."

"I saw him at a rodeo once. Probably about six years ago." The name had spurred her memory. "Everyone was talking about him. The poor cowboy who drew his name never had a chance."

"Well, Midnight's rodeoing days are long gone. He's a stud horse now." Sarah turned her attention to the open ledger on her desk. "I'm afraid I still do everything the old-fashioned way. The kids did buy me a slick-looking computer for Christmas a few years ago, but I have to admit I never took the time to learn how to use it. I have a laptop in the house that I use for my emails and surfing the web looking for good deals on livestock."

Leah looked over the computer. She'd love to have a newer model like it. "The computerized accounting packages can seem daunting at first. But I guarantee, once you're set up, they take a lot less time." Leah noticed some schedules next to the ledger. She picked them up. "Are these for the bank?"

"Yes. I need to file a cash-flow statement with them every quarter. This one is due on June thirtieth." Sarah ran her fingers through her stiff gray hair. Leah could sense the older woman's blood pressure rising just looking at the columns of numbers.

"If we got you computerized, you could print off these schedules in a flash," Leah promised.

"Really?"

"Yes, but I'd need to take a closer look at your records to give you an accurate estimate of what the conversion would cost."

"Could you possibly get started on that now? I'll be glad to watch over your children for a few hours. It's a beautiful day to play in the pool."

It seemed to Leah that Sarah couldn't get out of the office fast enough. For all that the older woman clearly didn't enjoy bookkeeping, Leah found the records in reasonably good order. Even so, it would be a big project to get everything computerized. Leah turned on the desk calculator and started punching in numbers, hoping that the final cost would be something that Sarah Hart found reasonable.

She was just finishing up her job estimate when she sensed a presence at the open door. She knew it was Colt before she looked. She could feel the electricity in the air, little prickles dancing on her scalp, her face, her hands.

"What do you think?" His voice, deep and warm, took her right back to the bar, to the moment when he'd sat next to her and she'd felt the brush of his shoulders against hers. "Can you handle the job?"

"I think I'm up to the challenge." She let her eyes raise to meet his, and despite steeling herself to remain calm and friendly, she had to admit that it would be a heck of a lot easier if he wasn't such a sinfully attractive man.

COLT HAD BEEN OUT helping trim the bucking stock's hooves in preparation for their next rodeo when he'd heard Leah's truck pull into the yard. It had taken a surprising amount of willpower not to run out to greet her. Instead, he'd focused on his job, finished and cleaned up in the barn before coming to check on her.

He found himself wanting to distract her from her books. "Ready for a break? How'd you like to see the future of this ranch?"

"You must be talking about Midnight Express." She glanced at the photo that the family had collaborated on for this year's Mother's Day gift. He'd been meaning to hang that for his mother. But right now, it seemed more important to show Leah around.

"None other."

"I would love to see him. But your mom has my kids and I should get back to them."

"This will only take a few minutes." He went behind her chair, which was on wheels, and rolled her out from behind the desk. Then he spun her around so they were face-to-face.

Those beautiful eyes of hers were going to be his undoing. He had to stop looking at her this way. Had to remember the parameters she'd set up for their friendship—and the very good reasons why he had to stick to them.

"Colt—"

"You're going to love this horse," he promised, taking her hands and pulling her up from the chair. She rose willingly, but immediately dropped his hands and stepped away from him once she was standing.

"I already do love Midnight," she told him, looking a little smug. "We met at the National Rodeo Finals about six years ago."

"I remember that year." He'd been on the sidelines watching during Leah's event. She'd ridden well, been less than a second shy of prize money on the last day. They'd bumped into one another at a bar later on that evening and he'd bought her a beer.

They had a lot of history, him and Leah. Funny that,

until two nights ago, he'd never seen her as anything but a friend. And now—he held the barn door open for her, appreciating the snug fit of her jeans as she walked by—he couldn't see her as anything but a woman.

"Midnight's over this way." As they cut across the yard, they chatted about some mutual friends, and he stumbled over a few of his words, distracted by the way the sunshine brought out flashes of red in her long, dark hair.

"I've lost touch with most of the old rodeo crowd," Leah admitted.

"It's tough to keep close ties in a profession with so much travel."

"Do you ever get tired of it? The travel, I mean?"

"Sure I do."

"Ever think of giving it up?"

"Impossible. Rodeo is the one thing I'm good at. And, as I already mentioned, the money's not bad, either." He stopped as they reached Midnight's corral. Leah put a boot up on the first rung of the fence, then hoisted herself to a sitting position. He did the same, leaving a healthy couple of feet between them.

About thirty yards away, Midnight laid back his ears and regarded them suspiciously.

"Gosh, he is one fine animal, isn't he?" Leah whistled with appreciation. "But who's the mare?"

"Her name is Fancy Gal. We bought her off the McKinleys and Midnight took a real shine to her."

"Love is blind, huh?"

"I guess Fancy Gal has what Midnight wants. She'll be having his foal next spring, Ace figures. Of course, so will about thirty other mares. Good thing Fancy Gal isn't looking for monogamy."

"Life is easy when you're a horse."

He wondered what she was thinking of when she said that. Her ex-husband? There must have been some real hard times leading up to their divorce. He didn't like thinking about any man hurting Leah. Didn't like thinking about Leah and other men, period.

"I don't think that's true in Midnight's case. His original owner passed away a few years ago and his kids left the animals in care of a real bastard of a foreman. Midnight was in pretty rough shape when we bought him."

The stallion twitched his ears and Colt had the eerie feeling that Midnight was listening, that he somehow *knew* he was the topic of conversation.

"Ace figured he could doctor him back to his former glory, and he's come close. But Midnight is still difficult to handle. Ace wants to be able to breed him under controlled conditions and so far that just isn't happening."

"Maybe he's like you—built for rodeo."

"I've wondered the same thing," Colt admitted. He wasn't looking at the horse anymore. How could he, with Leah just a few feet away from him? She looked so natural and pretty, perched on the fence like she belonged to this place. "What about you. Do you miss the old days, too?"

Leah hesitated. "I miss our farm," she finally conceded. "But not barrel racing. I have other priorities now."

"Your children."

"Exactly." She jumped gracefully to the ground. "Speaking of which, I'd better go find them before they drive your mother crazy."

Chapter Six

Leah found her kids at the side of the pool, being toweled off by Sarah Hart. They were all in bathing suits, though Sarah had covered hers with a caftan. Jill said something that made Sarah laugh and Davey started hopping from one foot to the other, the way he did when he was really happy.

"Mommy!" Davey came running for her as soon as he saw her. She scooped him up, then hugged his cool, damp body close.

"Did you have fun in the pool?"

"Mrs. Sarah taught me to swim. I do-ed it, Mom. All by myself."

"He sure did." Sarah held up a pair of water wings and winked at Leah.

Jill moved in closer and gave her a hug, too. "It's so nice here, Mom. They have a tire swing and a jungle gym set, too." She stepped back and looked at Colt. "Are you a real cowboy?"

Colt tipped his hat and nodded. "At your service, ma'am."

"Where's your horse?" Davey wanted to know.

"My mother doesn't allow horses in the pool."

Jill frowned, then gave a little giggle. She wasn't sure what to make of Colt, Leah could tell. She gave her daughter's shoulders a squeeze. "Colt's an old friend of mine, honey."

"Is he a friend of Daddy's, too?"

Leah glanced at Colt, then away. "No."

She gathered her kids' towels and folded them neatly next to the backpack. Sarah passed her the bottle of sunscreen. "Thanks, Sarah. It sounds like Jill and Davey had a terrific time. I hope they weren't too much trouble."

"Not at all. I had as much fun as they did, I suspect. You'll stay for lunch? I made lots of sandwiches this morning. The tray is in the fridge."

"I'll get it, Mom." Colt hurried into the house, as if glad for the opportunity to escape.

"That's very kind, Sarah. Maybe we'll have a quick bite, but we should leave soon. I need to check on my mother and make sure she's had some lunch herself." Once Colt returned with the food, she passed her children each a sandwich, then relaxed onto a vacant lounge chair with her own lunch. Davey curled up beside her, resting his head against her chest.

"I had a good look at your records," Leah told Sarah. "I'm familiar with a system called Farm Biz that I think would meet all your accounting and reporting needs. I've left an estimate on your desk for what it would cost to get you started with that. If you want, I could create an Excel spreadsheet to keep track of your bucking stock commitments, too."

Sarah asked her a few questions about the program and how it would work. Leah tried to answer as clearly as possible, even though she could tell the conversation was boring her children. Davey finished his sandwich, then snuggled up closer to her and closed his eyes. On the lounge chair next to hers, Jill lay back on a dry, plush towel.

"What about monthly updates?" Sarah asked. "Would you be willing to come out to the ranch to work on those?"

"Of course."

"That sounds wonderful, Leah." Sarah pushed her sunglasses up on her head, and gave her a warm smile. "You don't know how happy it makes me to know I'll never have to balance those accounts again."

"Does that mean you're giving me the job?"

"I will look at the estimate first, but I'm pretty sure the answer will be yes."

Leah knew she was beaming; she couldn't help it. With Thunder Ranch as her client, she knew others would soon follow. "Thanks so much, Sarah. For the job, and lunch, not to mention watching my children. I really should get them home now."

"It looks like they're fast asleep. Why not let them nap a while longer? Maybe you and Colt could go for a trail ride."

The idea was tempting, but Leah didn't dare even look in Colt's direction. He'd been hanging back during her conversation with his mother, gulping down his lunch like it was a job he was hoping to finish as fast as possible. Indeed, he'd made good work on it—the plate was empty now.

"I really shouldn't. My mother wasn't feeling well this morning and I want to check on her. The kids will sleep in the truck."

Slowly she eased off her lounge chair, holding Davey secure in her arms.

Sarah glanced at her son. "Colt, why don't you carry

Jill and the children's pack? I'll run back to the office and get Leah's briefcase for her."

Colt moved to the chair where Jill was sleeping. Leah watched as he gazed uncertainly at the sleeping child. Finally, he picked her up, holding her away from his body, as if she were an unsavory package.

Mentally shaking her head at him, Leah carried her son to the truck and settled him into his car seat. As she'd suspected, Davey didn't even open his eyes. Jill, however, woke briefly as Colt dumped her awkwardly onto her booster seat.

"Mom!" she cried, taken aback at being carried by a virtual stranger. Colt reacted by stepping back and raising his hands, as if to say, *What? I didn't do anything!*

"Excuse me." Leah motioned him out of the way, then gently strapped her daughter in and passed her a blanket. "It's okay, peanut. Just go back to sleep."

After shutting the door, she leaned her back against the sun-warmed metal. Colt was standing with his hands stuffed into the pockets of his jeans, looking uncomfortable.

"You're really awkward around kids."

"No kidding."

"They aren't creatures from another planet, you know."

"Hey. I have my reasons for feeling the way I do."

"What's that supposed to mean?"

Colt looked surprised, as if he'd blurted out something he hadn't meant to say. "Maybe one day I'll tell you." He glanced toward his mother, who was walking briskly toward them with Leah's briefcase in hand.

Leah didn't know what to say. He had her curious, that was for sure. But with his mother about to join them, she wouldn't try to pry anything more from him. Not now, anyway.

WITH THE KIDS SLEEPING soundly in the truck beside her, Leah drove slowly back to Roundup, hoping they'd get enough rest that they wouldn't be too cranky when they arrived at Grandma's. She resisted the urge to drive out for a look at their old farm. She didn't think she could bear to see it being occupied by another family.

The last time she was there had been for the auction, when her mother sold off the livestock and farm equipment, prior to putting the property up for sale. That was a day she would never want to relive. Seeing Country Girl sold to the highest bidder had almost broken her heart.

Jackson had been with her then, they'd been newlyweds and she'd hoped that if he saw the land, how beautiful it was, she might be able to convince him to become a Montana farmer, rather than take the high-paying job on the rigs he'd just been offered.

But Jackson hadn't seen the place the way she had. All he focused on were the problems—the barn that needed replacing and the fence that was falling down. "I can't imagine living in a house like this," he'd said when she'd taken him into the farmhouse kitchen.

The kitchen in their Calgary home had granite countertops, brand-new appliances and a gleaming hardwood floor. "But look out the windows," she told Jackson. "That view. All this space and clean air. Isn't that worth something?"

She hadn't really expected him to fall in love with the place. But she had hoped.

It didn't happen, though. Two days later, they were back in Calgary, she to prepare for the baby that would be coming in five months and him to start his first job rotation up in Fort McMurray.

Leah was driving slowly, so it took almost half an hour for her to reach town. As she reduced her speed, first Jill woke up, then Davey.

"Did you have a good nap?"

Jill rubbed her eyes and nodded. "That cowboy carried me, Mommy."

"Yes, I know." She waited to see if Jill had any further comments on Colt, but she didn't.

"We're going to check on Grandma now, okay?" Leah turned left off the highway, soon arriving at her mother's house. She helped the kids out of the truck, then they all trooped inside. Leah was relieved to find her mother at the kitchen table, eating some soup and a sandwich.

"I'm feeling so much better," Prue said, after giving the kids a hug. "How did your meeting with Sarah Hart go?"

Leah allowed herself a smug smile. "I think I got the job."

Before her mother could congratulate her, the phone rang. Since Leah was closest, she answered the call, her voice guarded in case this turned out to be her ex-husband.

It was.

"Leah. I can't believe I'm actually hearing your voice. You're a hard woman to track down."

"We've been real busy lately, that's for sure. But I'm glad you called, Jackson. The children would love to speak to you."

"Daddy?" Jill perked up as soon as she heard her father's name.

"Sure I want to talk to them. But can't we talk for a while, first? How's it going for you, Leah?"

His voice flowed like sweet, sticky honey, but Leah wasn't fooled. If it hadn't been for the two little faces looking up at her so hopefully right then, she would have hung up on the spot.

"I'm fine and so are the kids. How are things with you?"

"Lonely. I miss you."

Damn him for doing this to her. "And the kids miss you, too. Here's Jill. She's dancing on the spot waiting for her turn on the phone." Leah handed the receiver to her daughter. "Let Davey talk when you're finished, okay, peanut?"

She had to leave the room then. Just a few minutes to collect herself, that was all she needed. But unfortunately her mother couldn't give her that much space.

"You were awfully abrupt. Was that really necessary?"

Leah blinked away tears of frustration and anger. "Mom, whenever Jackson gets me on the phone, he tries to convince me to come back to him. It's not fair to the kids. They need him to focus on them—not me."

"What the kids really need is for their mother and father to be together again. I've offered before, and I'll offer again. Leave the kids with me, go back to Calgary and see if the two of you can't work things out."

"Mom. We're beyond that point. The divorce is final. We haven't lived together for over a year."

"You keep saying that. But lots of couples go through troubles, separate, then get back together. Mary Jo and Frank—"

"Mom! Daddy wants to talk to you again!"

Leah sighed, then put her finger to her mouth, warn-

ing her mother to drop this subject. Last thing the kids
needed was to hear the two of them fighting about
Jackson. She went back to the kitchen and asked Jill if
Davey had his turn to talk to his dad. When Jill nodded, Leah took the receiver—and a deep breath—then
spoke briskly. "Thanks so much for calling, Jackson.
The kids really enjoyed talking to you."

"When will I see them?"

She hated the whining note in his voice, and had to
work to ignore it. "Where are you? In Calgary?"

"No, up north. Working."

So why ask to see them, when it wasn't even pos-
sible? Again, Leah struggled to be calm and logical.
"Well, let me know when you get your next break and
I'll be glad to drive them up to Calgary for a visit."

"Maybe you all can stay with me?"

Leah carried the phone into the living room, away
from the watchful eyes of her mother. "The kids, yes.
Me, no."

"Leah—"

"Stop it, Jackson. I really can't take this anymore.
We've said everything there is to say. Nothing can
change what happened, or how I feel. I have to go now.
Please call to talk to Jill and Davey anytime you want.
But not me. Leave me the hell alone."

THE NEXT MORNING Colt was up early again, feeding the
bucking stock, when his older brother strode up to the
corrals. Ace was the tall, dark and handsome one of the
Hart boys, but he'd never used his good looks to charm
the ladies the way Colt had. At heart, his brother was
quiet, solid and dependable. Colt figured Flynn had
made herself a fine catch.

Colt set aside the pitchfork and offered Ace his hand. "You're back. How was the honeymoon?"

"Fantastic. Too short, but fantastic." Ace hesitated only for a second before accepting his handshake.

"I have to admit, you look like a happy man. I'm glad for you, Ace. And—" Colt swallowed, then choked out the rest "—and I apologize for not being here to be your best man. It meant a lot that you wanted me and I'm sorry—" He swallowed again.

Looking back he realized he should have forgotten about his meeting with old man Mackay. He'd really wanted to come home with that contract all sewn up and impress his mother and Ace with his amazing negotiating skills. But Brad Mackay had wanted to talk to his wife first, before agreeing to anything. And so Colt had come home with no contract, and no memories of his brother's wedding, either.

"We didn't give you much notice," Ace conceded. "But when I finally got Flynn to agree to marry me, I had to act fast. No way was I giving her time to change her mind."

Colt laughed, then grew serious again. "I still want to make it up to you. If there's anything I can do—"

"Well, now that you mention it…"

"Uh-oh." Seeing the wicked gleam in Ace's eyes, Colt realized he might have been smart to tie some strings to his offer.

"Since Flynn and I are going to be living on her property now, I need to move some stuff. There's a couple chairs in the tack room Mom said were just collecting dust, and she has an extra dining room suite in the basement she said we could use, too. Want to help me load everything into the truck?"

Another move. Was his body ever going to get a

chance to rest and recover? Colt shook his head rue-
fully. "No problem. Give me twenty minutes to finish
here, then I'm all yours for as long as you need me." He
hesitated. "Is Flynn here?" He really should apologize
to his new sister-in-law, too.

"She wanted to come, but I talked her out of it. Last
thing I want is for her to be lifting and carrying things."

Colt glanced away at this reference to Flynn's pregnancy. Ever since his brother had shared the news of the
upcoming baby, he'd wondered what his brother would
say if he knew the truth about Colt's past. A few times
he'd even been tempted to blurt out the whole story. But
then there'd be one more example of how Ace had done
the right thing and Colt had done the exact opposite.

Ace clapped him on the shoulder. "I feel a lot better
with the air cleared between us."

Colt swallowed. He wished he could feel better, too.
But it seemed everywhere he turned he was reminded
of just what a mess he'd made of his life.

TWENTY MINUTES later Colt was ready to help his brother.
Ace had backed up one of the ranch trucks to the front
of the barn, and Darrell had propped open the doors at
both ends so they could move the chairs from the tack
room straight into the truck. Colt was carrying one of
the heavy oak chairs when Leah showed up wearing a
blazer and skinny jeans tucked into her boots. Colt had
to admire the way she combined business and Western
wear, managing to look sexy, competent and smart all
at the same time.

"Hey there." He set down the chair in order to say
hello. "You're here to work?"

It felt so good, just to see her. He had to admit she
still got his heart racing, despite their agreement to be

only friends. But there was something decidedly un-friendly in her eyes today. They didn't have their usual warm sparkle. In fact, she looked darn-near somber.

"Yup, it's my first day and I want to get right at it. Mom's got the kids for the morning so I'm hoping to get a lot accomplished. What's going on here?" She nodded at the truck.

"Ace is moving a few things over to the McKinley spread." At that moment his brother came out of the barn carrying a large box. Ace set it into the truck then came and offered his hand to Leah.

"I know you. Didn't you used to compete in the barrel races with Dinah?"

"That's right, I did. And you're obviously Colt's older brother, Ace."

Colt could tell Leah immediately liked Ace. Not surprising, but still a little annoying. He put a friendly arm around her shoulder. "Leah and I were in the same year at school. Known each other forever."

"Oh, so I don't need to warn you to watch out for my sweet-talking brother?"

Leah laughed and slipped out from under his arm. "Colt and I figured out a long time ago that we were never meant to be more than friends."

Well, didn't she say that easily, as if she'd never been tempted to want anything more. Colt was finding this conversation increasingly irritating.

"By the way," Leah added, "congratulations to you and Flynn on your marriage. I hope you'll be very happy."

Ace nodded. "Thank you. I'm sure we will. Especially since we're expecting a baby around Thanksgiving. I can't deny I'm a very lucky guy."

"Well, isn't that nice." Leah deliberately looked from

Ace, to Colt. "A man looking forward to the responsibilities of being a father."

Colt glared at Leah. That had been a low blow. A really low blow. He picked up the chair and pretty much hurled it into the back of the truck.

"Easy there, bro." Ace looked surprised and perplexed. "I was hoping to use that chair again. Not throw it in the junkyard."

Leah just shrugged, then headed for the office.

Chapter Seven

Leah worked hard all week, determined to focus on what mattered: being a good mother and provider for her children. Colt had been driving her crazy ever since that night they'd hooked up at the Open Range. She knew she had to stop thinking about him, or she'd end up making another major mistake, like Jackson. The fiasco that had once been her marriage was a vivid reminder of what happened when she allowed herself to fall for the wrong sort of man.

She spent Tuesday and Wednesday mornings at Thunder Ranch, while her mom babysat. In the afternoons, she took the kids out to explore their new town. They scouted out the local playgrounds, went down to the river to throw rocks and play poohsticks. On Wednesday afternoon she put them in the wagon, then walked downtown, hoping to post notices advertising her accounting services. She'd already booked an ad in the *Roundup Record Tribune*, but that wouldn't be out until next week. Sierra at the Number 1 Diner and Austin Wright at his Western Wear and Tack Shop were both gracious about allowing her to use their bulletin boards.

While in Wright's shop, Leah stopped to admire a belt much like the one Sarah Hart had been wearing.

Then she noticed a pair of earrings that would work beautifully with her wardrobe. As she touched them, a woman came up behind her.

"Those are forty-five dollars. The setting is pure silver and the stones are genuine amethysts."

"Cheyenne?" Leah was surprised to see Austin's younger sister. Like her, Cheyenne had done some barrel racing in her past. Her striking red hair had made her a standout with the fans. "I thought you'd moved to California?"

"I did...." Cheyenne barely managed a smile. "But I'm back home now." Two little red-haired girls, obviously twins and just a little younger than Jill, came out from behind the counter. One of them wrapped her arms around Cheyenne's leg and Cheyenne placed her hand protectively on her head. "These are my daughters—Sammie and Sadie."

"Aw, aren't you two the cutest! I have kids now, too." Leah put down the earrings. She'd buy them as a special treat for herself if she managed to land a second client. "Jill and Davey." She pointed to the wagon she'd parked inside the store, near the front, with warnings to stay put and eat the lollipops she'd bribed them with. Since she rarely gave them sugary treats, they were being pretty cooperative.

But she could see them eyeing Cheyenne's girls curiously.

"Our kids might enjoy playing together. We should get together for coffee sometime," Leah suggested. Cheyenne had changed in the years since she'd seen her last. She'd once been so sure of herself, outgoing and friendly. Now she was still friendly, but it was almost as if her personality had been muted.

Cheyenne nodded. "That would be nice. Maybe on the weekend?"

"Sure. My phone number is on the poster I just hung over there." She pointed to Austin's bulletin board next to the cash register. "We don't need much notice, just give us a call when you have some free time."

SINCE MONDAY, Colt had gone out of his way to avoid Leah. On Tuesday he went out with his cousin Beau, riding the cattle that were grazing in the south pasture. They'd taken two young quarter horses that were in need of some on-the-job training, and had separated from the herd a heifer with watery eyes for Ace to examine.

Wednesday Beau had other business, but Colt went out prowling again. He needed the alone time to clear his head and do some thinking. Leah was on his mind for a lot of that day.

He'd been attracted to many women in his life, but he'd known from the moment he'd spied her in the Open Range Saloon that what he felt for her was different. The attraction between them had been almost magical—until she'd told him about her kids.

It was one thing to think he might be ready for a committed relationship with a woman he loved. Quite another to contemplate being part of a family of four. But while his head told him they were wrong for each other, his heart just wouldn't listen.

Leah had left the door open to being friends. Maybe if he started with that, he would see the way to the future more clearly.

So on Thursday, Colt stuck near to the ranch, cleaning out pens and hauling hay until about an hour before Leah usually left the ranch. Then he rolled three barrels into the big dirt arena they used to train horses and set them up in the prescribed triangular pattern, counting out strides to estimate the distance between them. When he was done, he headed to the office.

Leah was filing some papers when he walked in. She had her back to him as she stuffed a folder into the top drawer. Suddenly she went still.

"Colt, is that you, again?"

"I didn't mean to sneak up on you. I promise."

"It's uncanny how you keep managing to do that, all the same."

He took a casual step inside the office, and glanced around. There were several neat stacks of paper on the desk, some of them quite high. "How's it going?"

"Really good, actually. I'm making faster progress than I'd hoped."

"Good. Maybe you can take a little break, then?"

She frowned. "Why would I want to do that?"

"Come on. Isn't there any room for fun on that schedule of yours?"

Her eyebrows arched skeptically. "That depends on what you mean by fun."

"I've set up the barrels and saddled Dinah's old palomino for you. The one she used to use when she was in junior barrel racing."

"Are you kidding me?"

Colt could tell she was intrigued. "Come on, give it a go. Just for old times' sake. You can't tell me you haven't missed being on a horse."

"It's been so many years. My timing will be way off."

"So? Doesn't mean you can't have some fun."

Leah looked at the stacks of paper on the desk. Then at him. Suddenly she smiled. "What the heck. Lets give it a try."

LEAH REMOVED her blazer and hung it on a fence post. The sun was almost directly overhead and she smiled gratefully when Colt placed a white Resistol hat on her head. She adjusted the angle a fraction of an inch, then nodded. "It's a good fit."

"I figured you for a six and three-quarters, like Mom."

She turned away from the warmth in his smile. *Just friendship, Leah,* she reminded herself. *We're just out here having a little fun, and that's all.*

"You look the part," Colt said. "Now it's time to meet your horse." He went into the barn and came back with a beautiful light-caramel mare with a long-flowing mane the color of ripe barley.

"She's still gorgeous," Leah breathed.

"Buttermilk Biscuit is getting old now, but I think she still knows what she's doing."

Slowly Leah approached the palomino, letting the horse get a good look at her, and a good sniff, before she stroked the side of the horse's head. "That's a good girl, Buttermilk. You see those barrels out there? You want to give those a try?"

Buttermilk nickered and tossed her mane. Leah laughed. "I do believe we speak the same language." She checked the length of the stirrups and the cinch belt, then walked around the horse, patting her and talking gently.

"You may be old but you're in good shape, aren't you, Buttermilk?"

"Since she was elected sheriff, Dinah hasn't had much time to ride her, but Mom makes sure Buttermilk gets her exercise."

"Your sister is the sheriff?" Leah positioned the reins in her left hand, then slid her boot into the stirrup and swung herself up into the saddle. Buttermilk stayed beautifully in position, and Leah patted her neck. "I didn't know that."

"Yeah, it's a surprise given all the trouble she got into as a kid. But she likes the job. And I hear she's good at it."

Leah urged the horse forward, walking for a bit, then loped around the arena a few times. She could tell that Buttermilk was eyeing the barrels. The old horse knew what she was really out here to do.

Colt had left the arena and was sitting up on the fence near the first barrel. Judging from his wide grin, she was doing okay so far.

Leah urged the horse into the correct position, lining her up to an imaginary point about twelve feet inside of the first barrel. The money barrel some people called it, because if you didn't get this one right, your whole ride would suffer.

Leah had intended to walk Buttermilk through the routine for the first try, but Buttermilk was having none of that. As soon as Leah gave her a little nudge and loosened the reins they were off. They took the first barrel a little wide, and Leah had to adjust. The second barrel was better, though Leah's leg nicked it slightly as Buttermilk came up around the back. Then they were off for the third and final barrel. They were way too wide on this one, but Buttermilk still raced home as if a championship ribbon was on the line. Colt whooped as they crossed their imaginary finish line.

"Not too shabby!"

Leah was laughing. What a hoot. She really had missed riding, much more than she'd realized. She cantered Buttermilk over toward Colt and was about to thank him for setting this up, when Ace walked by.

"You two seem to be having a good time."

Colt lost his grin real quick. "Just having a little fun."

"Excuse me. I've got a sick heifer to look after." Ace brushed past his brother. "If only fun could pay the bills around here."

"Hell, Ace. Loosen up a little, would you?"

Ace just shrugged and kept walking toward his clinic.

Leah slid off the horse, suddenly feeling guilty. But she charged by the hour and the only one paying for this bit of foolishness was herself. "I'm sorry. Maybe this wasn't such a good idea."

"Don't worry about Ace. I thought I smoothed things over with him the other day, but apparently not." Colt took the reins from her hand. "I'll take care of Buttermilk. You better get going. I know you like to be home for your kids before lunchtime."

Leah felt guilty leaving the work to him. But he was right. The deal she'd worked out with her mother was that she would watch the children for three hours in the morning, then Leah would take them home for their lunch and naptime.

She removed her hat, exchanging it for the blazer she'd left on the fencepost, then glanced back at Colt, catching him off guard. He immediately grinned and gave her a wink, and she wondered if she'd imagined the look of longing she'd glimpsed before he knew he was being watched.

AT THE DINNER TABLE that evening, Leah was shocked when Jill asked, "When are we moving back with Daddy?"

Leah set down her fork. "Peanut, I explained to you about divorce, right? I won't ever live with your daddy again. This is my home now. But you and Davey will be able to spend time with your dad, sometimes, when he isn't busy working on the oil rigs. It'll sort of be like having *two* homes for you and Davey."

Jill shook her head. "That's not what Grandma says."

Leah pressed a hand to her forehead, feeling an ache coming on. "Did Grandma talk about this today?"

Jill nodded. "She talks about Daddy a lot. She says we all belong together because we're a family."

Oh, good Lord. How could her mother do this to these poor children? They were so young, and already very confused about the whole divorce thing. It was one thing for her mother to speak her mind to Leah, who was an adult, after all. But quite another to drag the kids into this.

"Well, I'm sorry. Grandma is right about a lot of things, but not about this."

Jill fattened her bottom lip. "That's not fair, Mommy. You're being selfish." She pushed her plate of carrots and chicken away. "I don't like this. I want to go to Grandma's house. She has better food."

"Me, too," Davey said. "Grandma makes good fwench toast."

Leah stared from one child to the other, momentarily lost in a morass of parental quicksand. Guilt washed over her, and for a second she felt that everything Jill was saying to her was deserved. She *had* been selfish. She *hadn't* put them first.

But then reason kicked in. Damn it, she hadn't had a choice—Jackson hadn't left her one. Sure it was painful and hard, but this fresh start was necessary. She had to be calm and she had to be firm.

"Jill, you need to apologize for calling me selfish."

"But that's what Grandma says."

Really? Leah's heart sank. Was that how her mom saw her? And how could she blame her child for parroting the very words she heard from her grandmother?

It was a lot to think about, and Leah was silent for the rest of the meal. The children picked up on her mood and didn't speak much, either.

Leah watched a TV program with the kids after dinner, then they went through their usual evening routine as if nothing had changed. But when Jill and Davey were finally tucked into bed and sleeping, she took the phone into her bedroom and shut the door. Sitting on the edge of her bed, she inhaled shakily, then made the call and relayed the conversation she'd had with her children.

"Well," her mother huffed. "You can't blame me for putting words in their mouths. You're the one who's ruining their lives by tearing their family apart."

She couldn't mean that. "I told you Jackson cheated on me. Did you expect me to put up with that?"

There was a long pause. Then, "Sometimes women have to make sacrifices for their families. I'm sure Jackson regrets his mistake."

"Are you? And even if he does, have you thought about what it would be like for me? Separated from Jackson for months on end while he works up north? It was hard enough when I thought I could trust him." She hated that her mother was making her dredge up all these old memories and emotions. Living through those awful times had been difficult enough. She'd moved here because she needed to make a new life for herself and her children. But her mom wouldn't let her do that.

"Over time it would get easier, Leah."

Oh, crap! She couldn't take this anymore. "Mom, I appreciate everything you've done for me and for the children. But until you're ready to accept that my divorce is final and stop giving my children hope that Jackson and I are going to get back together again—"

"What?" her mother cried in alarm. "Are you telling me I can't see my grandchildren anymore?"

"No, of course not. I just want to be around when you do. So I can vet what you say to them."

Click. Her mother hung up the phone, so Leah couldn't finish the rest of her thought.

And it's not fair to me, either, Mom. Aren't you supposed to be on my side?

THE NEXT MORNING Leah told the kids that they were coming with her to work, but that they would have to play quietly and not interrupt. She packed along activity books, toys and the portable DVD player, hopeful that she could get at least a couple of hours of work done before they became too restless.

This was just a stopgap solution, though. She needed to make new child-care arrangements. Maybe Cheyenne would have some suggestions. Tomorrow was Saturday. She'd give her a call and see if she was free for that coffee they'd discussed.

No one was around when Leah pulled into Thunder Ranch at nine o'clock. She led her children through the yard, to the barn.

"Can we please play in the pool?" Jill lagged, her gaze on the sprawling ranch house.

"Want to swim!" Davey agreed.

"I'm sorry, but we can't use the pool, unless we're invited. This isn't our house. I'm here to work, remember?" Leah pulled the toys and activity books out of the pack and set them on the office floor. "You guys play with these for a while, and then you can watch a DVD, okay?"

They weren't often allowed to watch shows during the daytime, so the bribe was effective. Davey grabbed a fat crayon and a Thomas-the-Train coloring book. Jill preferred pencil crayons and a farm-themed activity book.

Finally Leah settled at the desk and resumed entering data into the new accounting program. It wasn't easy to concentrate, however. Not only was she keeping one eye on the children, but her own brain also kept trying to distract her, too. One second she was rehashing that awful argument with her mother. The next she was thinking about Colt, wondering where he was working today and if he might pop in for a visit, and maybe mention something about the weekend?

It was foolish to think this way. He was all wrong for her, and they both knew that. But they'd had so much fun yesterday in the riding arena. The more time they spent together, the more she liked him. *Really* liked him.

Forty-five minutes went by before the kids started getting restless. A Winnie-the-Pooh DVD bought Leah another forty-five minutes. But the credits were no sooner rolling, than Davey came crawling onto her lap. "Mommy, can I help?"

Jill started wandering around the room. She stopped at a bronze trophy depicting a saddle bronc rider. "What's this, Mom? Can I play with it?"

"Leave that alone, Jill. And I'm sorry, Davey, but you can't touch the keyboard. This is Mommy's grown-up work."

"I'm bored." Jill made a second lap around the office. "I want to go swimming, or play on the swing...."

"Swimming!" Davey agreed.

With a sigh, Leah saved her work, then shut down the computer. "I've already explained that this isn't our house and we can't do those things unless we're invited. But how about we go for a little walk to visit the horses before we go home?"

"Sure," Jill agreed quickly, and Davey fell in with his sister. Leah packed their belongings and her brief-case into the truck, then, with a firm hold on each child's hand, took them around the back of the barn. She thought she'd show them Midnight. And if Colt happened to be working in the pastures close to home… well, she supposed that would be okay, too.

Turned out she found them both in the riding arena. Leather rigging had been cinched around Midnight's girth and Colt was lunging him, calling out encouraging words as the stallion cantered in a wide circle around him.

"That a boy, Midnight. Let off a little steam and then I have a surprise for you."

"Horse!" Davey said, excited, pointing to the black stallion.

"Is that Midnight, Mom?" Jill clambered up the first rung of the fence and even so, could just see over the top. At that moment Colt noticed them, too. He removed his white working hat and waved it at them, his face breaking out in a happy grin.

Leah propped Davey on the second rung of the fence, keeping both of her hands on his waist as she leaned in closer. What was Colt up to? She noticed Gracie come out of the barn and settle on the fence to watch. Gracie was too far away to speak to them, but she waved at the kids and they waved back.

About five minutes later, a second ranch hand showed up and settled next to Gracie.

"You planning to run that horse in circles all day there, Colt?"

"Just warming him up, Darrell."

Colt was in faded jeans today, well-worn boots and a shirt that looked to have faded from blue to almost-white. Every item of his clothing was molded to his lean, muscular frame and Leah, who had seen a lot of cowboys in her life, couldn't recall ever seeing one who was better-looking than Colt.

No wonder the guy got into so much trouble. He was too damn irresistible for his own good.

But he was dependable when it came to horses, Leah conceded. There was no doubt in her mind that he'd established a connection with Midnight. The stallion changed directions willingly at Colt's signal and that, in itself, was something. Then, finally, Colt stopped moving, and let his arms fall to his side. He turned his back to the stallion and made a show of slowly walking away.

Midnight trotted up behind him, like a tame puppy dog.

Colt was close enough now that Leah could see the twinkle in his eyes. He gave her a wink, then turned to face the horse. "Hey there, boy. You ready to be my friend now?"

Colt walked slowly around the stallion, then grabbed a safety vest that had been hanging over the fence and slipped it on. Clearly he intended to ride the stallion, and Leah found herself leaning in even closer to the action.

Midnight had been born to buck. Did Colt really think he could ride him? Maybe the Harts had decided Midnight should retire from the rodeo. But that didn't mean Midnight felt the same way.

She watched as Colt maneuvered the horse closer to

the fence. Darrell came up from the other side and took hold of Midnight's bridle.

"Easy, boy," Darrell said, as Colt climbed the rungs of the fence, leaning a little of his weight onto Midnight's saddle as he maneuvered into position. Next Colt wedged his left hand into the rawhide rigging, then eased off the fence, swinging his leg over Midnight's back and sinking down until all his weight was on the horse. For a second Midnight seemed confused.

Colt patted the side of his neck. "Wasn't expecting that, were you, buddy?"

And then Midnight got feisty.

Chapter Eight

Midnight jumped so high, both Jill and Davey let out startled gasps. Within seconds, Colt was having one of the wildest bareback bronc rides of his life. No need to spur this bronc into action, Leah thought, as Midnight bucked his way into the center of the arena. Then he turned in a wicked corkscrew that catapulted Colt right over the stallion's head.

Colt landed on his butt in a cloud of dirt.

Both Darrell and Gracie burst out laughing. Davey's eyes were as big as a Canadian dollar coin. Jill tugged on Leah's belt loop. "Is he okay, Mommy?"

Leah had had one heart-stopping moment as she'd watched Colt flying through the air. But his quick jump up, and dusting off of his jeans, soon had her relaxing.

"He's just fine, honey. This is what rodeo cowboys do. You've seen the videos of your daddy before he went to work on the oil rigs, right?" Jackson had specialized in the bareback event, too, which could be summed up as follows. Cowboy rides wild horse. Cowboy ends up on his butt in the dirt. Leah couldn't explain why the event had such an enormous appeal to audiences, but she was as captivated by the spectacle as anyone.

Colt was laughing as he headed toward them.

"That was some ride," Leah said, feeling the smile on her face getting wider and wider, the closer he came.

"Sure was," Colt agreed. "I'm not sure who had more fun. Me or Midnight."

The stallion was circling the arena, snorting, head held high. If horses could smirk, Leah was sure that's what the stallion would be doing.

"Well, we know who the winner was anyway." She pointed to her watch. "You didn't come close to lasting eight seconds."

"You're right about that." Colt didn't seem upset at all that he'd been bested by the horse. In fact, he seemed almost gleeful. He turned back for another look at Midnight. "You know what I think?"

"Go ahead and tell me," Leah teased. As if he wouldn't.

"That horse has one true calling. And it's the rodeo."

"Well, duh."

"Trouble is, Ace won't let him go back."

"And this is only Ace's decision to make?"

Colt looked at her thoughtfully. "Good question."

COLT HAD TO ADMIT IT. Leah and her kids made a pretty picture gathered together on the pasture fence. Something about the way Davey leaned his weight back on his mom especially moved Colt. But he also noticed Jill's hand latched onto her mother's belt loop, even as she leaned as far over the fence as she dared.

Leah's kids were cuter than average, he figured. They both had their mom's thick dark hair, fair skin and deep blue eyes.

Right now, all three sets of those eyes were looking at him.

"Were you scared when Midnight started bucking?" Jill asked.

"Scawed?" Davey parroted.

"Mostly it's exciting. But I am a little bit scared, too," Colt admitted. "Don't tell anyone, okay? Cowboys aren't supposed to be scared of anything."

He glanced at Leah, who was the picture of a proud mama, beaming down on both of her children as if they were the greatest treasures on the earth.

The oddest feeling came over him, an ache deep in his chest, as he thought about another mother, and another child.

Hell. He had to stop doing this to himself.

Leah was looking at him oddly, so he guessed he was revealing more in his expression than he'd intended. He'd better get out of here before he did or said something really dumb. But just as he was thinking of a quick exit line Jill hit him with another question.

"Do all horses buck like that?"

Sensing her anxiety, Colt was quick to be reassuring. "Not at all. Horses like Midnight are born for the rodeo—born to buck. But we have other horses on Thunder Ranch that we breed to be good trail riders and to work with cattle. Some of them are as gentle as can be." He could see the sparkle of interest in her eyes. "Would you like to meet one of those horses?"

"Maybe." Her voice was cautious, but Colt could see the longing in her eyes.

Leah could, too. "I believe I have a budding horse-lover on my hands. Colt, are you sure you're not too busy?"

"It's almost time to break for lunch, anyway. The horse I want to show you is called Glory Days." He started toward the shaded corrals behind Ace's clinic in the horse barn.

Jill ran up beside him and he shortened his stride so the little girl could keep up. Leah, holding Davey on one hip as if he weighed as much as a down pillow, came up beside them.

"So how old were you when you started riding?" he asked her.

"About Jill's age," Leah confessed. "My dad taught me and by the time I was seven, we'd go out riding together."

"Did you have cattle on your farm?"

"Yes, for milking. We also had chickens and a few pigs."

They'd reached the corral and Colt spotted Glory Days munching on hay pellets near the fence. He whistled, and the old quarter horse lifted her head. When he pulled a treat out of his shirt pocket, she started ambling in their direction.

"Hey, girl," he cooed, breaking in two one of the special horse cookies that were hand-baked by Angie Barrington, the owner of the local animal rescue shelter.

Glory knew the cookies well. She munched down on the combination of oats, carrots and raisins, then bumped Colt's chest with her nose, looking for more.

Colt passed the other half to Jill. She checked with her mom and after getting a nod of approval, climbed up the fence so she could offer the treat to Glory.

"Just hold your hand flat," Colt advised her. "Glory only eats from the finest of dinnerware."

Jill giggled, whether from his comment, or the tickling sensation of Glory feeding off her palm, Colt had no idea. But it was a happy sound, all the same.

At that moment, Ace emerged from his office. "Mom

just called. She's serving lunch out on the patio and she's invited Leah and her children to join us."

PLATES OF SANDWICHES and veggies had been set out on the table by the pool. "Nothing fancy," Colt's mother said, as she'd fussed over Jill and Davey, making sure they were sitting in the shade of the patio umbrella, then cutting the crusts off their sandwiches, even though Leah tried to tell her it wasn't necessary.

Ace and Flynn were sitting side by side across the table from Leah and her children. Sarah sat to Ace's left, leaving Colt next to Flynn.

Everyone was hungry and the food went quickly. When Flynn offered to go into the kitchen to prepare dessert, Colt volunteered to go with her. This was his opportunity to say he was sorry to his new sister-in-law and she was gracious enough to accept his apology.

"Our wedding was pretty last-minute," she said, kindly.

"Well, I'm still kicking myself in the butt for not making sure I was there on time. Though even if I had been, I doubt Ace would have noticed. From what I hear, he only had eyes for you."

Flynn laughed. "Oh, you are a sweet-talker, aren't you?" She handed him a bowl of grapes. "Rinse these, would you? I'll slice some cheese to go with them."

"What about those cookies on the counter?"

"We'll take those out, too. I'm sure the kids would love some, and so would I, to tell the truth. I wasn't too hungry at the beginning of my pregnancy," she confided, cutting off a large slice of the cheddar. "But suddenly I'm ravenous."

"Well, you're looking great," Colt said honestly. He'd known Flynn all his life and had never seen the pretty blonde looking better. Of course, he reflected as they carried the platters back outside, happiness could have something to do with that.

While Leah, the kids and Flynn tucked into the dessert, Colt asked his mother and Ace if he could have a quick word.

"I tried riding Midnight today," he said without preamble.

"I heard the ruckus," Ace said. "Leah and Jill were just filling us in on the details."

"Yeah, well, did she tell you that Midnight is about the most talented bucking horse I've ever had the pleasure to not ride?"

"She did. And I don't know why you were foolish enough to try. What if Midnight had been injured?"

"Midnight?" Colt slid his hat back on his head. "Believe me the only one in any danger out there was me." He turned to his mother, hoping she'd be more sympathetic. "That horse had so much fun. I think he's missing the rodeo. And we're missing out on the huge money we could be making by adding him to our bucking string."

His mother never got a chance to answer. Ace was so angry he tossed his hat on the ground. "Are you kidding me? You know how much we paid for that horse. He's a stud horse now, not a bucking bronc. And we can't risk him getting injured."

"Stud horse, huh? Then why haven't you been able to breed him under controlled conditions? Ever thought he needs to let off some steam?"

"That's crazy, Colt. One thing doesn't have anything to do with the other."

"How do you know?" Colt stepped in close to his brother, his chest pumped, hands fisted. "How much time have you spent on the back of that horse?"

Ace closed the distance between them so they were separated by less than a foot. "About four seconds less than you from what I heard."

"Enough, boys!" Sarah pushed them apart, then stepped between them. "I will not have you arguing this way. Especially in front of the children."

Ace picked his hat up from the ground and dusted it off. "As soon as Colt drops this ridiculous rodeo idea, we'll have nothing to argue about."

Colt glanced back at the table, where he could see Leah eyeing him anxiously. "I'll drop it—for now." He'd concede this battle. But he was determined to win the war.

DAVEY FELL ASLEEP shortly after lunch was over. His head was on Leah's lap and she sighed, thinking she should have loaded them into the car sooner. Jill looked sleepy, too, but she was bound and determined to go for a swim. She just kept staring at the pool, hoping to get an invitation. And finally it came.

"Did you bring your swimsuit, Jill?" Sarah asked her. She'd made coffee after the intense conversation between her sons. Ace and Flynn had gone back to work at the vet clinic, but Colt had stayed for a cookie and a cup of coffee. Now he was watching her and the kids with a pensive look in his eyes.

Leah wondered what he was thinking. And if she'd get a moment alone with him in order to ask.

"It's in the car, Miss Sarah." Jill had perked up at the question.

"Well, why don't you get it, dear. You can have a little play in the pool while your brother sleeps in the shade." She turned to Leah. "Unless you have some-place you need to go?"

"Not really."

"Well then. Why don't you and Colt go for a trail ride since you couldn't the last time? Davey looks like he's out for an hour, at least, and Jill and I will have no trouble amusing ourselves, will we, dear?"

Jill's eyes widened. "Please, Mom? Please say we can stay."

The plan was falling almost too neatly into place. Leah glanced at the moody cowboy sitting in the shade about ten feet from her. "I'm sure Colt has other things to do—"

"One of them is to check the fence out along Thunder Creek. I promised Uncle Joshua I would make sure it was secure since the water is getting so high." He tilted his head in her direction. "Pretty country for a trail ride…"

Leah needed no more tempting. "My rubber arm is twisted. Could I please ride Buttermilk again?"

ONCE THE HORSES were tacked up, Leah and Colt rode for almost twenty minutes without feeling the need to talk. Leah wasn't sure she could. A bittersweet joy had welled up to fill every spare inch of her body. God, she had missed this. Thunder Ranch wasn't her old farm, but the countryside was so familiar: the gently rising hills patched with sage-green ponderosa pine and fresh-leaved aspen, the wild grass cluttered with white wild daisies and purple asters, magenta lupines and yellow bitterroot.

Even the color of the sky and the shapes of the clouds spoke of her childhood and home, and all the things that had once been comforting and familiar to her.

At a few places where the fence sagged, Colt slowed his mount, a sturdy, nut-brown quarter horse he called

Atticus, and made markers using the GPS function on his phone. He'd be back tomorrow, he said, to make repairs.

A good idea, Leah reflected. The muddy spring water in the creek was living up to its name, thundering from the glacier capped mountains in the distant Rockies toward Musselshell River—the very river that flowed past her new place.

They slowed their pace a second time when they came upon a yearling that had lost the herd. Colt laconically circled his lariat above his head, and then the circle of rope was flying through the air, landing square around the bewildered little guy's head.

"Come on, don't fight it," Colt advised the yearling. "We'll help you find your momma."

Leah hadn't seen signs of the herd so far. "Any idea where they are?"

"Yup. I was out riding the other day with my cousin Beau. Not that much farther," he reassured her. "Once we make that rise over there, we should see them on the other side."

Now that they were traveling more slowly, it was possible to talk.

"This is so great, Colt. Reminds me of all the wonderful times I had with my father as a kid. I took it all for granted back then, as if I would always have my dad and a horse and a hundred acres at my disposal."

"Did your mother ride, too?"

"No. She never took to it. I think she was nervous of the horses, and the cattle, as well. She was happy to stick close to home with her chickens and the garden." Leah guided Buttermilk around a fallen tree. "Did you do a lot of riding with your father?"

"Not so much. He was closer to Ace."

Leah could hear the hurt in those words. "Second child syndrome, huh?"

"Oh, I didn't make it easy on my dad. I was always pulling some stunt or other, getting in trouble and making him play the role of disciplinarian. Meanwhile good-as-gold Ace just kept on being the perfect son. Like he still is now."

"What do you mean by that?"

"Oh…everything. He's a vet and he has his own business, as well as helping Mom with the ranch. Now he's married and about to become a father, too." Colt shrugged. "He does it all, and makes it look so damn easy."

"You have a lot of accomplishments, yourself. You're an amazing competitor—tie-down roping, steer wrestling, bareback bronc and bull riding. Some would say you do it all, too."

"I may have won All-Around Cowboy a few times, but there's more to life than rodeo."

"Did I really hear you say that?"

Colt laughed. "So they tell me. Say…why did you bring the kids with you today? Did your mom have another headache?"

Leah hesitated, then decided she needed to talk to someone, why not Colt? She knew he'd keep their conversation to himself. "Actually, we had an argument. The same damn argument that sent me running to the Open Range the other night."

"Something to do with your ex?" he guessed.

"Yeah. She wants me to get back with him. I don't mind so much when she brings this up with me. But I found out last night that she's been telling the kids that their daddy's moving home."

Colt pulled his horse to a halt. "Why would she do that?"

Leah signaled Buttermilk to stop, too. "Wishful thinking. But it's not fair to the kids to make them hope for something that will never happen."

She met Colt's gaze and wondered what he was thinking. Next thing she knew he asked, "What happened, Leah? You get such a hurt look on your face when you talk about him."

Leah shifted her gaze to the softly undulating Bull Mountains to the west. "No one expects marriage to be easy—not with divorce rates the way they are. When Jackson decided to quit the rodeo and go to work in the oil rigs in northern Alberta, I supported his decision, not realizing how little time he would be spending at home. We could have made it, though, if I hadn't—"

She paused. She'd told her mother the details, but no one else. It wasn't a tale that was easy to repeat. On the other hand, this was Colt, and there were things she wanted him to understand.

"About two years ago, Jackson had a weekend pass. Not enough time for him to travel all the way to Calgary, so he decided to spend the weekend in Edmonton. I had a neighbor back then, a responsible, wonderful woman who babysat for me occasionally. She volunteered to take Davey and Jill so I could join him. It was supposed to be a surprise."

Colt got a worried look. "I take it you were the one who got the surprise?"

Chapter Nine

"I'd call it more an ugly shock than a surprise," Leah said. "Jackson had been seeing this woman for over six months, whenever he had a few days that he could slip away from the job."

Colt swore. "Poor excuse for a man."

"He told me I should understand. That it was harder for him to deal with our long separations than it was for me, because I had the children."

"Sorry. Can't see the logic in that."

"Me, either. I wish I could have believed that he missed Jill and Davey, but even when he was home, he rarely made time for them. He was always keen for me to hire sitters so we could go out partying at the Ranchman's like the so-called *good old days.*"

She'd been pretty disappointed in Jackson's lack of parenting skills, especially when she compared him to her own dad. But she'd never thought about leaving him until she'd found out about the cheating. And even then, she'd given him a chance, agreeing to talk to a counselor before making a final decision.

"Jackson took a leave of absence and we spent a few months in therapy. But it wasn't any use. The anger and the hurt that I felt…maybe I could have dealt with those. But I'd lost respect for the man I'd married. He'd been sneaky and amoral and I just couldn't see him as my life partner anymore."

"No one could say you didn't try."

She tried to smile. "My mother says it all the time. But I truly felt like I had no other alternative when I finally asked Jackson for a divorce."

"You made the right decision."

Leah felt a sudden rush of emotion that had her blinking back tears. "It feels so great to hear you say that."

After more than a year of defending herself to her mother, finally someone was validating her decision.

"Seriously, Leah, what else could you have done but leave him?"

"Thank you. I think so, too. But my mother has been on my case so hard lately, I was starting to doubt myself."

"Well, don't." Colt nudged his mare until she moved right up to Buttermilk. Then he reached over to squeeze Leah's shoulder. "You deserve better."

She swallowed at the intense look in his eyes. She couldn't believe how relieved she felt after finally confiding all the details of her divorce to him. He really was a good man. A much better man than he gave himself credit for, she thought.

And there could be no doubt that something powerful was building between them, despite all that talk about being "just friends." All she had to do was look in his eyes to know he felt it, too. Maybe now that he'd met her children, and had time to adjust to the fact that she was a mother, they could give this thing between them a real try.

After this afternoon, she really felt it was possible.

COLT WOULD HAVE happily stayed out riding with Leah all day long. But once they'd reunited the stray yearling with the herd, he could tell her thoughts had turned to her children and that she was anxious to get back to them. Instead of following the meandering creek, they took the direct route home.

Leah dismounted gracefully, but with a grimace. "I'm going to pay for this tomorrow." She rubbed her butt with both hands, then lamented. "I used to be able to spend a whole day in the saddle, no sweat."

"Cowboy up, Stockton. You've grown soft." Actually she'd impressed him with how well she'd ridden after so many years of city living.

He reached for her reins. "Here, I'll take care of Buttermilk. Go ahead and rescue your kids from my mother before she decides to kidnap them."

"More likely they're driving her crazy by now. But it doesn't seem fair to leave you with all the work, either." She followed him into the barn, then when the horses were in their stalls, she unfastened Buttermilk's cinch belt.

"I don't mind." He'd do a lot more—for her. But how could he tell her that? Would she even give him a chance? He figured there was a reason she'd trusted him with the details around her divorce from Jackson. That had been her way of telling him a man had let her down once and she didn't want to go through that again.

Not that he would ever hurt her the way Jackson had.

But there were other ways of hurting a woman.

Once they'd removed the saddles, he led the way to the tack room.

"Wow, look at this. You have so much space in here." Leah set the saddle she'd used onto the bench for cleaning. "Everything is so organized and well-maintained." She ran a hand over the most expensive saddle on the ranch. "This is one of your cousin Beau's, isn't it?"

"It is. Mom commissioned it as a Christmas surprise for my father a long time ago. Cattle prices were high and we'd had a very good year. She said he was always providing for his family, it was time his family did something nice for him." Colt ran a hand over the well-worn leather, too. "Since he passed, I don't think anyone has used it."

"I wonder what it's worth?" Leah was still inspecting the fancy scrollwork.

Not Colt. He was inspecting Leah. The ride had brought color to her cheeks and a glow to her eyes. He'd thought she was beautiful when he saw her at the bar last weekend. But now he had a new appreciation for the woman she was inside. She was strong, but she'd let him see that she could be vulnerable, as well.

He moved his hand closer to hers, until the tips of their fingers were touching.

"Colt?"

He held her gaze for a long moment, and when she didn't move away, he did what felt completely natural, almost inevitable. He kissed her.

This kiss wasn't like the ones they'd shared that first night. Those had been about passion and instant attraction, whereas today and right now was about so much more.

He kissed her so she would know that he wanted her to be his, that she could count on him, that they were meant to be....

And she kissed him back the same way, sighing a little as she leaned her body into his. He touched the soft silk of her hair, the warm skin of her neck. She smelled of all the things he loved—fresh air, grass, horses...and woman.

He wrapped his arms tightly around her and deepened their kiss, circling her waist with his hands, then sliding his hands down to her butt and pulling her in nice and close.

She went up on her toes, tilted her head, then drew back a fraction of an inch. "We're doing it again…isn't this against our agreement?"

"I was hoping there might be a loophole…?" She was driving him mad. Absolutely mad. Her body up against his, her hands on his back, her moist, warm lips a breath from his.

"No loopholes. No fine print." Her words were tough, but she was still in his arms, and her face was still a delectable few inches away.

"Well then, let's toss the whole agreement in the trash, where it belongs. Leah, I can't fight this anymore." Staying "just friends" with this woman simply wasn't possible.

"I still have two kids. And while I admit this feels very nice—" she kissed him lightly on the lips, pulling back before he could make it into something more "—I can't get more entangled with you until I know you're good with that."

He hadn't forgotten about Jill and Davey, of course. Only it was so easy to imagine them out of the picture when they were being taken care of by someone else. "They're great kids," he said slowly.

Leah tilted her head, clearly not happy with his response. A second later, she slipped out of his arms. "I can tell that they like you, though Jill may have her reservations. But you were surprisingly good with them today." She crossed her arms over her chest and he knew she was waiting for him to tell her that he liked her kids, too, and that their existence in this world was no longer a deal-breaker for him.

In some ways, saying those words would be easy. The truth was, he'd surprised himself by how natural he felt around her kids. Perhaps he wasn't as hopeless as he'd thought he would be.

But even if that were true, he still had his past to deal with. She'd been honest and open with him today. She deserved the same courtesy from him. But could he do it? Tell her the secret that he hadn't shared with anyone else in the world?

He had to try.

Gently he cupped her face between his hands. "We need to talk, Leah, but not here. Would it be all right if I came by your house later tonight, after your children are sleeping?"

LEAH WAS DYING TO know what it was Colt wanted to talk about. But she had to respect his request that they leave the subject until later that night. At his insistence, she left him to finish with the horses. Back at the ranch house, she thanked Sarah profusely, then loaded her children into her truck.

Back in Roundup, they were driving past a playground, about a mile from their home, when Jill pointed to a mother pushing two little girls on swings.

"That's your friend, Mommy. The lady with red hair."

Leah took her foot off the gas pedal and glanced to her right. Indeed, there was Cheyenne and those two cute girls of hers. "Want to stop and play for a while?"

She wasn't surprised when both kids gave her an enthusiastic "yes." She pulled to the side of the road, then freed the children from their car restraints. Both headed straight for the swings, a long setup with five bucket seats made for smaller children.

"Hey, there. I thought I recognized you in your truck." The wind was playing havoc with Cheyenne's long red hair, and she tucked it back behind her ears.

"Beautiful day to be outside, isn't it?" Leah introduced Cheyenne to her children, then helped Jill and Davey climb into the swing seats. For a while all four children were happy to be pushed by their mothers.

"So, have you had any responses to your poster?"

"Not yet," Leah admitted. "I'm trying not to get discouraged. It's only been up for a couple of days."

"I'll say you shouldn't be discouraged. Several of the phone numbers have already been torn off from the bottom of the sheet you tacked up at Austin's shop. I'll bet you'll start getting lots of calls soon."

Leah was encouraged to hear that. Computerizing the accounts at Thunder Ranch was taking most of her available time for now, but in another couple of weeks, she'd be needing more work.

"Can I get out now, Mommy?" one of Cheyenne's twins asked.

"Sure, Sadie."

After that, all of the other kids decided they'd had enough swinging, too. Leah helped first Jill, then Davey, down to the ground. Jill headed straight to the twins. "Do you want to play with me and my brother?"

The same little girl who had asked to get out of the swing first nodded yes, then took Jill's hand and started leading her to the climbing equipment. Davey and the other twin followed silently behind them.

"Your daughters look so much alike. I'm struggling to tell them apart," Leah admitted.

"If she's talking, it's probably Sadie," Cheyenne said, settling on a bench close to the children.

Leah sat next to her, her gaze on the quieter twin.

When Davey followed behind his sister, climbing up the wooden stairs that led to a platform and a couple of slides, Sammie held back. She kept looking from the other children, to her mother.

"Was Sammie always the quiet one?"

"More so since her father died."

"I'm so sorry, Cheyenne. He was a marine, wasn't he?"

"Yes. He wasn't killed in active duty, but Iraq killed him all the same."

Cheyenne's expression was flat, but tears were pooling in her luminous green eyes. Leah struggled for the right words to say, but in the end just reached for one of Cheyenne's hands and gave it a tight squeeze.

"How are you doing now?"

"We're trying to make a new life here in Roundup. It's so different from California, but the girls are adjusting. California may have wonderful weather, but Montana is home."

"I feel exactly the same way. Plus, it's good to be close to family." Leah sighed. "At least, most of the time it is."

"Oh?"

Leah explained about her breakup and divorce from Jackson, and the issues she'd had with her mother since coming home. "This week everything came to a head and I told Mom she couldn't babysit anymore unless she refrained from talking to them about their father. She wouldn't. So now we're at this big impasse and I'm stuck without a babysitter for my kids. Do you know of anyone I could hire?"

"Actually, I do. Jessica Crane works part-time at the Number 1. She even has a business card." Cheyenne dug one out of her purse and passed it to Leah. "I was hoping to leave Sammie and Sadie with her so I could spend more time working on my jewelry, but Sammie becomes so upset anytime I mention it, that I haven't dared, yet."

Leah accepted the card gratefully, then gave a ten-minute warning to her children. "This has been really nice, Cheyenne. We'll have to get together again, soon."

"I'd like that. It's good to talk to someone who understands." Cheyenne told the twins that it was time they headed home, as well.

As the two groups went their separate ways, Leah reflected that she'd done most of the talking, while Cheyenne had glossed over the years she'd spent in California and her husband's death. Judging by the pain that floated so close to the surface in Cheyenne's eyes, there was a lot more to the story.

Back at home, Leah showered the children, and herself, then cooked pasta for dinner. Later they played marathon rounds of Trouble before Leah read them their bedtime stories and tucked them under their covers. Finally, at nine o'clock, they fell asleep.

Leah sent Colt a text message: Kids sleeping. Come anytime.

His answer was immediate. On my way.

Leah couldn't relax. The kitchen was already spotless. She put away the board game and the books, and rearranged the cushions on the sofa about ten times. Then she went to the bathroom and checked her image in the mirror. She was lucky to have thick hair that dried naturally into flattering layers. Not usually one for makeup, she decided to apply a little mascara and lip gloss. The final result was not half-bad, she thought. Especially for a working mom of two.

Now what? Maybe she should put on a pot of coffee?

She heard a knock at the door.

He was here. She felt herself smiling as she went to open the door. And there he was. Standing on her front step wearing pressed jeans and one of his nice red shirts, tucked in to show off the buckle on his belt. *All-around cowboy...*

He certainly was.

"Well." He looked over her shoulder. "May I come in?"

He seemed nervous. "Of course." She stepped aside to make room for him, and only then noticed that he'd brought a bottle of wine.

"Should I open that?"

"Good idea. Unless..."

"Would you prefer a beer?"

He smiled his relief. "I was going to bring over a case, but it just didn't seem as classy." He set the Shiraz on her kitchen counter, then gratefully accepted the cold bottle she'd removed from her fridge. She opened a second one for herself.

"Since when do you worry about being classy?"

"This was probably the first time," he admitted.

Colt started pacing the small kitchen, like a nervous stallion sensing thunderstorms in the air. All afternoon Leah had speculated on what he wanted to tell her. Seeing how tense he was now, she started to feel nervous, too.

"Want to sit outside?" They would both do better in the outdoors, she thought, and Colt was quick to nod his agreement. They left the kitchen door open and headed to the small patio where she had a couple of plastic chairs her mother had given her.

Some of the kids' toys were strewn around, including Davey's plastic riding tractor. More reminders of the two children who were such a big part of her life. Any man she loved would have to be capable of loving them, too.

Leah settled in one of the chairs, but even out here Colt couldn't seem to stop pacing. She took a deep breath and tried to be calm. It was only now dusk and the sky had mellowed into a beautiful pale lavender. Beyond the fence she could see the fast flowing Musselshell, whose banks had risen at least a foot since they'd moved in. The snow should be off the mountains by now, so hopefully the river had reached its peak.

"There's something I need to tell you. Something I've never told another living soul."

Leah forgot about the river. Colt had all her attention now. The poor cowboy was so worked up. She wished she could do something to make this easier for him. "Just say it, Colt. You know you can trust me."

He stopped pacing then. Feet planted shoulder-width apart, he faced her straight on. "Today, when you said that your kids liked me—well, I like them, too. In fact, I'm surprising myself with how much I like them. But my situation…it's more complicated than that. I have obligations—financial obligations—that make me leery of having a family of my own, or even getting involved with a woman who already has children."

She felt more confused than ever. "What kind of obligations are you talking about?"

The look in his eyes now was close to anguish. He seemed to be struggling to find the right words. And finally he blurted out, "Child support payments."

Leah's brain went numb. She stared at him as if he'd spoken to her in Mandarin. Then slowly the words, and their meaning, came into focus for her.

Support payments were paid by parents. The conclusion was obvious. "You mean you have a child?"

"Yes. A son."

Chapter Ten

"You have a kid? A son?" If she repeated it often enough, maybe the meaning would finally sink in. Leah stared at Colt, wondering if she'd ever really known him. How could something this big lie in his past without her having had a clue?

"I do." Colt had turned away from her and was gazing out toward the river, fists jammed into the pockets of his jeans. He looked, Leah thought, like a defeated man.

"Who's the mother?"

He didn't answer at first. Then he sighed. "Janet Greenway. I met her at the rodeo in Belt, outside of Great Falls. We spent a few nights together. Then I moved on."

The story of his life, Leah reflected. *Then I moved on.*

"When did you see her again?"

"I didn't. Nine months later I received a registered letter from an attorney telling me I'd fathered a child and would be required to make child-care payments."

"Really? She didn't call you before that?"

"Really." Colt lifted his head briefly, then returned to the view. "She didn't want to talk to me, and didn't want me having any part of her life or the baby's. Apparently she'd met someone new about a month after our…affair. They fell in love and he agreed to raise her son as his own. So they got married."

"Wow." This was a lot to take in. Part of her had to sympathize with what it must have been like for Colt, to find out he was a father by registered mail from a law firm rather than the mother. But then, looking at it from the woman's point of view, Colt had never bothered to contact her again after they slept together. So what did she really owe him?

"I gather you weren't invited to be present when the baby was born. So when did you first get to see him?"

"I didn't. I haven't."

"What?"

"According to the lawyer, all Janet expected from me was a financial commitment. The baby had a mother and a father. My presence in his life would only have complicated matters."

"But…that's hogwash. You had rights, too…."

When Colt didn't say anything, Leah realized that while he may have had rights as a father, he hadn't chosen to exercise them.

She hadn't known what he was coming here to say, but secretly she'd hoped that it would be something good. Something that would offer hope that the two of them might have a future, that along with Jill and Davey, they could become a family, share their lives and grow old together.

But this. This made a mockery of the whole idea.

Her voice trembled as she said, "The arrangement suited you, too, didn't it? That's why you didn't fight her."

"The kid had a father. He didn't need me."

She marched across the patio and grabbed his shoulder, wanting to see his eyes. "You can't believe that."

"It's the truth."

"Maybe you wish it was. Because this way, your life hasn't had to change a bit, has it?"

"I've never missed a child-care payment."

"Well, good for you, Colt. I suppose you're real proud of yourself for that."

"I'm not saying I'm proud, only that it hasn't been easy. Since we've been expanding at Thunder Ranch, I've forfeited my salary and had to count on rodeo winnings for everything. Which explains why I'm thirty-two years old, still living in a twenty-two-foot trailer and, until I won big in Oklahoma, driving a truck that was almost fifteen years old. Hardly makes me a good catch for a woman with two kids, huh?"

"Money. Is that really all you think this is about?"

THE SCORN IN Leah's voice was coming through loud and clear. Colt wasn't surprised. He'd expected nothing else.

Of course he knew this was about more than just money. But that was the piece that was easiest to single out. Maybe he should have kept his mouth shut. But saying the secret out loud had been an unexpected relief. Finally, he was facing the thing that had been eating him up for so many years.

In the beginning it hadn't been too hard to put the existence of his son out of his mind. He paid the checks once a month, but other than that, he didn't think about it much.

He expected that, over time, the complicated, achy ball of emotions that rolled around in his chest every time he wrote that check would get smaller and smaller until finally it disappeared.

Instead, the opposite happened.

Each month he felt worse, not better. One year turned

into the next. Nothing changed in his life. He kept rodeoing, moving from town to town, with occasional pit stops at the ranch. Lots of late nights spent in bars, or the bedrooms of women he didn't know very well. Doing his best to avoid serious conversations with his father, mother or older brother. Knowing that if he told them the truth about himself, they'd lose whatever respect they still had for him.

Until he'd arrived at this place, now, where he'd finally found a woman he felt he could spend his life with, only to discover he wasn't good enough for her.

He could see it in her face when she looked at him. He flinched, and turned his eyes to the view of the evening sky.

"What's his name?"

His throat choked over the word. He tried again. "Evan."

"He must be what—twelve years old?"

"I guess."

"You guess." He could hear the anger rising in Leah's voice. "And you've never seen him, to this very day?"

"No."

It sounded awful now, even to him. But what alternative had he had? He'd done what Janet wanted him to do, trusting she would make the right choices for the boy. They both had known he had nothing to offer the kid, beyond the financial.

Colt hadn't realized that the temperature had dropped until he noticed Leah shivering. He fought the impulse to wrap his arm around her. "We'd better go in."

"Actually, you should just leave." She pointed to a path that led around the side of the house to the front. "Shut the gate behind you, okay?"

"So this is it? We're done?"

"What you've just told me confirms that you were right from the beginning. We're both looking for different things in life. That doesn't mean we can't be friends. Honestly, I can't imagine not being friends with you, Colt. But we have to draw the line there."

She sounded sad, but very, very sure. He'd thought there were more things to say. But Leah, apparently, didn't agree. He'd been tried and found guilty.

The verdict, Colt reflected, as he stepped off the patio, boots sinking in the packed dirt path, was hardly surprising.

As COLT DROVE AWAY from Leah's house, he wished, desperately, that he had a rodeo booked for the weekend. He didn't want time to replay their conversation over and over in his head and he sure didn't want to think about what had happened twelve years ago. He wanted to forget the entire mess and the best way to do that, in his experience, was to risk his neck on the back of a bucking horse or a raging bull.

You couldn't be thinking about anything but the present when you were competing at a rodeo. Best of all, he usually won something, which almost always made him feel better about himself. For a while…

Colt swore. At himself. At the world.

Resisting the urge to drive to the bar, he headed for home instead. He'd get up early tomorrow and fix that fencing. When he was done, maybe he'd give the tack room a good cleaning. He'd noticed today that it could use one.

Trouble with ranch work, though, was that while it taxed the body, it left the mind with too much time to think. He remembered his father once saying that ranching was the perfect life for a man who was comfortable in his own skin.

"You spend a lot of time with no one for company but the land and your horse," he'd said, "and if you aren't on good terms with yourself, the hours pass mighty slow."

The advice had been rare, and the occasion even rarer…a family trail ride with Mom and Dad, Ace, Dinah, Tuf and himself. His mother and Dinah had ridden ahead for some reason and his father had been speaking to just the boys.

Tuf had been young back then and hadn't really understood. "Why wouldn't a person be on good terms with themselves, Dad?"

Colt recalled his father's answer. "I hope you never find out, son."

That advice had been one of the main reasons he hadn't felt able to go to his father for counsel when he got that letter from Janet's attorney. He'd known instinctively that this was exactly the sort of mistake his father had been talking about. The kind that made living with yourself a very uncomfortable proposition.

Only later, after his father's death, had Colt learned that his father may well have been speaking about his own demons—a problem with drinking that he'd done his best to hide from his family. Maybe this weakness was what had made the old man so hard on his sons— not wanting them to make the same mistakes he had.

Colt leaned forward in his seat as he neared the ranch. He could see headlights in the drive, which puzzled him. Ace and Flynn wouldn't be working this late. Did his mother have company?

A few moments later he was close enough to see a truck idling near the barn, and as Colt approached, intending to park beside it, the driver blinded him with his high beams before hitting the gas and screeching out of there. Colt twisted around, but only saw red taillights as the truck disappeared up the road.

Now what the hell had that been about? He parked by the house and was almost at the side door, when his mother stepped outside.

"Was that you, Colt? Why were you driving like a maniac?"

His mother was in her pajamas and housecoat, and looked like she'd been sleeping. So whoever had been in the truck had definitely not been an invited guest.

"That wasn't me, Mom. I just got home and saw headlights so I thought I'd investigate."

"Well, if it wasn't you, then who was it?"

"It's Friday night, so it could have been kids out joyriding, I guess." He couldn't think of any other explanation. "Just in case, why don't you make sure to lock all the windows and doors tonight. I'll go out to the barn and check on the horses."

He kissed his mother good-night, then turned around and headed for the barn. The outdoor lights were powered by motion detectors and he had plenty of light to see by as he walked past his truck to the horse barn. He heard a few nickers and snorts—the horses clearly had been riled, but from what he could see, nothing else was out of the usual.

Colt circled the barn, checked Ace's clinic for signs of a break-in, since expensive medicine could be a target for thieves, then went back to the paddock to make sure Midnight was all right. The stallion was restless, sure enough. He raced from one end of the paddock to the other, then threw his head high and snorted.

"It's okay, buddy," Colt told the horse. "Whoever it was is gone now."

But just to make sure, Colt decided to sleep on a cot they used sometimes when they wanted to keep a close eye on a sick horse or a mare in the middle of a difficult delivery.

Maybe that truck driver had simply driven down the wrong lane by mistake and there was nothing to worry about.

But somehow, Colt didn't think so.

LEAH WAS IN BED, trying to read a book by her favorite author, but she kept having to go back and reread pages, which made her cross. She so rarely found some quiet time to read. Now that she had the chance, she couldn't concentrate.

Damn you, Colton Hart.

She was flipping back to the beginning of the chapter for the third time when she heard a bedroom door creak open, then footsteps padding along the hall.

Before she could jump out from under her quilt to investigate, her door swung open and Jill stepped inside.

"I had a bad dream, Mommy."

"Come here, peanut." Leah set aside the book and made room for her daughter. Jill was wearing the top to her pink flannel pajamas and the bottoms to the red Calgary Flames pajamas that her father had brought for her on his last visit before they moved to Montana. The braids Leah had put into her hair earlier that evening were now sticking out like Pippi Longstocking's. Leah thought her daughter looked totally adorable.

She wrapped her arms around her little girl and felt a flood of maternal love and contentment as Jill snuggled in next to her. Colt had no idea what he was missing, she thought. No idea, at all.

"Are you okay?"

Jill tightened her hold. "I dreamed about Daddy."

"Oh?" Leah brushed a hand over her daughter's head.

"I dreamed he was here. But he couldn't see me. It was scary, Mommy. Am I going to see Daddy again?"

"Yes, you will. I promise. As soon as he has some time off work, you, Davey and I are going to drive back to Calgary and you'll have a good long visit."

"A visit isn't the same."

Leah knew very well what her daughter meant. And it broke her heart. "I know. Maybe when you're older, you can stay with your dad longer and it will be like living with him again."

"But you won't be with us?"

Leah sighed. "No."

"That sucks."

She had to laugh. "Yes, in some ways it does. But the most important thing is that you know your dad loves you, and your mom loves you. Even if we can't all be together, that part doesn't change and will never change."

Jill seemed to relax then. She eased her hold on Leah and snuggled into the covers. "Can I sleep with you, tonight?"

"If you promise not to snore."

Jill giggled. "Did Daddy snore?"

Leah reached over to turn out the reading lamp. "A little."

"Does that cowboy snore?"

That cowboy? "You mean Colt Hart?"

"Yeah."

"I don't know, honey. Colt and I are just friends, remember?"

Oh, great. Jill might not consciously know why she'd

segued from a conversation about her father to one about Colt, but to Leah the answer was pretty obvious.

Double damn you, Colton Hart.

"WHY THE HELL are you sleeping out here? Have too much to drink last night and lose your way?"

Colt covered his eyes with his arm as his blanket was wrenched off his body. With a few succinct words he told Ace where he could go. "Give me back that blanket."

"No way. It's time you got up and got some work done. Maybe take a few painkillers, first."

"I don't need any painkillers." Colt pushed up into a sitting position, then planted his feet on the barn floor. Hell, he was still wearing his boots. No wonder he hadn't slept all that well.

"Mom said some joyrider was in the yard last night." Ace sat on a wooden chair next to the cot.

His brother, Colt reflected, looked rested, clean-shaven and well-dressed. Not one of those adjectives could apply to him right now. He tried to brush down his hair, which had a tendency to give in to cowlicks first thing in the morning. "That's why I decided to camp out here for the night. In case whoever it was decided to come back."

"Yeah?" Ace looked surprised. Then impressed. "Good call."

Praise from his brother was pretty rare. Colt worked at tucking his shirt back into his jeans in order to hide the pleased smile he couldn't hold in. "So why are you here? Don't you and Flynn have plans for the weekend?"

"We do in our alternate existence where we work regular nine-to-five jobs. Here in the real world, I have an emergency call to deal with. I was just heading to the clinic to pick up some supplies when I heard your snoring."

"Since I don't snore, that isn't possible."

"Right. Anyway, I'd better get a move on. Flynn's waiting for me in the truck." He headed for the door, then turned back. "And if you're looking for something to do today, there's tack that could use cleaning."

Usually, just the fact that Ace asked him to do something was reason enough for him to argue against it. This time, though, he just said, "Sure. I'll get right on it." He could fix the fences later in the day. It really didn't matter in what order he tackled the jobs, as long as they both got done.

Ace gave him a strange look, then nodded. "Good. See you later."

Well, how about that. An entire conversation with his brother and neither one of them had raised their voices. Colt decided to start on the tack room right away, and save breakfast for later. With last night's conversation still weighing down his gut, he didn't have room for food, anyway.

Only now could he admit to himself that he'd driven to Leah's last night with more than a little hope in his heart that Leah would be willing to overlook what had happened in his past. After all, he'd been twenty then. Just a kid. But apparently she wasn't inclined to be lenient, and given what she'd been through with Jackson, he supposed he couldn't blame her.

Colt crossed the barn to the tack room, and was surprised to find the door ajar because he knew he'd closed it yesterday. Possibly one of their hired hands had been in the room since then. But they would have closed the door, too, he was sure.

As soon as he stepped into the room, he realized something was very, very wrong.

The place was a mess. The wooden chest holding their most expensive reins and bridles was open, with tack spilled out over the concrete floor. Colt glanced to the right. The shelf normally holding horse blankets was empty. Even worse, the wall bracket for his father's saddle was empty as well.

Less than twenty-four hours ago he and Leah had both touched that saddle. Colt knew none of the hands would have dared moved it.

Everything clicked into place, then.

They'd been robbed.

Chapter Eleven

Colt ran to Ace's office. His brother was at the fridge, transferring vials of medicine into the black case he took with him on his calls.

Colt halted at the doorway. "I figured out what that truck was doing in our yard last night. Seems like we've been robbed."

"What!" Ace almost dropped the vial in his hand, recovering just in time.

"The tack room is a mess. I'm guessing I scared them off when I came home last night. They got quite a bit of stuff, anyway, including Dad's saddle."

"Damn it. That saddle was worth about twenty thousand."

"I know." Colt leaned against the door frame, still recovering from the shock of it himself. "What do you think I should do?"

Ace glanced impatiently at his watch. "Think you could figure that out on your own?"

Colt reared at his brother's tone. "Fine. I will. No need to bite my head off, Doc."

"Look, I'm sorry, okay? I was supposed to be out at the Emerson ranch ten minutes ago."

"Once they hear we were robbed, they'll understand if you're a few minutes late."

"If their cow dies, I doubt it." Ace closed his case and secured the latch. After giving a final look around to make sure he hadn't forgotten anything, he headed for the door. "Just call Duke at the sheriff's office, okay? He'll let you know what to do."

Colt followed his brother, stopping at the truck to say hello to Flynn before continuing to the house. He found his mother perched on a stool at the kitchen island with her laptop, sipping coffee while she perused an online listing of bucking stock for sale. He thought about the deal he was working on. At some point he'd have to talk to his mother and Ace about it, but this wasn't the time.

"Bad news, Mom. You know that truck we heard last night?"

She frowned and set down her mug. "Were they vandals?"

"Worse. Thieves." He told his mother about the missing tack.

"Oh, no. Are you sure your father's saddle is gone, too?"

"Afraid so."

She was silent for at least a minute, probably thinking back to the Christmas morning when they'd blindfolded their father and led him out to the barn to see his "surprise."

"It's a pretty distinctive saddle, Mom. Maybe we'll get it back when the thieves try to unload it."

"I hope so." Her mother looked wistful. "I don't mind so much about the tack. It should be covered by insurance, anyway. But I sure do hate the idea of losing your father's saddle."

"Good thing we have a sheriff in the family. Dinah will track it down." Colt pulled out his phone to give her a call.

His mother placed her hand over his phone. "Your sister's away on a course, remember? Duke's probably covering for her."

Duke, Dinah's deputy, was Beau's fraternal twin, but he was closer to Ace than to Colt. All the boys had grown up together on Thunder Ranch, since the death of Duke and Beau's mother when they were really young.

Their father, Joshua Adams, was Sarah's brother and she and John had encouraged Joshua to build a home for his boys on Thunder Ranch. After Sarah's decision to start the bucking stock business, Joshua and Beau had taken over the cattle and bull side of the operation. Duke still helped his dad and brother, as well as competing in rodeos and acting as the local deputy, which made him a very busy man.

"Okay," Colt said. "I'll give Duke a call. Meanwhile, could you pull out our insurance policy? I should probably follow up with them, too."

His mother looked at him with a mixture of surprise and relief. "That would be great. Thanks, son."

Colt was suddenly glad Ace had been busy and had left the theft for him to handle. He helped himself to a cup of coffee, scanning the counters for any sign of food, but his mother had obviously already cleaned up after breakfast. He sipped his coffee, then leaned against the butcher-block counter to think.

Maybe he should drive into Roundup and talk to Duke in person. After he filed his report, he could grab a bite at the Number 1, then take a casual drive past Leah's house.

TWENTY MINUTES LATER, Colt was in Duke's office, being guided through the necessary paperwork to report the theft. Once he was done, Duke assured him that he'd be out to the ranch within an hour to take some photos and check for fingerprints. "Did you happen to get a look at the truck?"

"The driver flashed his brights—pretty much blinded me."

"I'll see if I can get an impression of the tire treads."

"I figured you might do that, so I blocked off that area of the yard. Unfortunately Ace and I both drove our trucks right up to the horse barn before we knew there'd been a theft."

"I'll do castings of your treads to eliminate them. Hopefully we'll still find something from the perp," Duke said. "And we'll keep an eye out for any second-hand tack hitting the market. For sure the distinctive markings on Uncle John's saddle will make it easy to trace if the damn fools decide to unload that too close to home."

"Anyone who steals another man's tack is either desperate or foolish," Colt said. "Hopefully our guys belong in the latter category."

He got up from the chair, and settled his hat back on his head. Before he could leave, Duke asked if he was going to the Yellowstone Roundup in Gardiner next weekend.

"Planning to. Are you riding?"

"Yeah. I told Dad I'd help with the bulls, as well. We're scheduled to drive them down on Thursday."

"Okay. We'll see you then." Colt nodded his thanks then stepped out to the street. His stomach rumbled at the sight of the Number 1 Diner, reminding him he still hadn't had breakfast.

But as soon as he stepped inside, he forgot all about food.

Leah was here.

She happened to look up at that exact moment and he smiled, hoping she would do the same. God, she looked good, but then Leah always looked good.

"Hey there, Colt."

No smile. Not even a hint of one. At least she hadn't ignored him.

"You must know Cheyenne Sundell?" Leah continued. "She's Austin Wright's sister."

He turned to the redhead sitting with Leah, a pretty woman with sad eyes. Yeah, he remembered her all right. "You were a barrel racer, too."

"I was indeed. And you were the cowboy that all our mommas warned us against." She held out her hand. "Nice to see you again, Colt."

Leah gave him a pointed look. "For the record, Colt, Cheyenne has twin daughters." She glanced at the next table over, where Jill and Davey were sharing coloring books and crayons with two little red-haired girls.

Dirty blow, Leah. He ignored her and smiled at the girls. "You gals gonna grow up to be barrel racers like your Momma?"

One of them giggled. "That's Sadie," Cheyenne said. The other girl hid her face shyly behind her coloring book. "And that's Sammie."

"*I'm* going to be a barrel racer, Colt," Jill said. Her hair was in braids that stuck out from her head, and she was wearing a garish combination of pink top and orange vest.

"Is that right, half-pint? You'll have to learn to ride, first."

She nodded her head vigorously, which caused her braids to bob wildly. "You can teach me if you want."

Leah let out a combination laugh and groan. She murmured to Cheyenne, "Your daughters look so ador-

able. Jill fights me every time I try to suggest an outfit, and she only lets me touch her hair twice a week in
order to wash it."

"A mother has to pick her battles," Cheyenne said.
"My girls don't really care what they wear…yet."

Colt was glad that Leah allowed Jill to be herself.
He didn't care for women who fussed too much about
what their children were wearing. He'd once caught the
tail end of a show called *Toddlers and Tiaras* that had
scared him to death.

"Can we come to the ranch today, Colt?" Jill slid off
her chair and ran up beside him. "Davey wants to swim
in your pool and I do, too, but first I need to learn to
ride a horse."

"Jill!" Leah jumped up to usher her daughter back to
the table. "It isn't polite to ask for invitations. And you
promised me you would stay in your seat if we let you
kids sit together. Look at your brother. He's younger
than you, and he hasn't broken the rules."

Of course Davey had to pick that moment to make a
liar out of his mother. He came racing at Colt, holding
out his arms so Colt had no choice but to pick the little
guy up. The smile on Davey's face was pure delight.

They gave their affection so easily, Leah's children.
Colt's mood sobered as he suddenly appreciated why
she was so protective of them.

"Swim!" Davey said. "Wanch!"

"Wanch?" Colt looked at Leah for an interpretation.

"Ranch," she repeated, reluctantly. "I'm sorry, Colt."
She held out her arms and after a second's pause, he
passed the little boy back to her.

"You have to sit down, Davey, and let Colt have
his breakfast. Look—here come your pancakes." She

smiled at the young waitress who came laden with four plates from the children's menu. "Thank you so much."

Colt stood awkwardly to the side for a few moments as both Leah and Cheyenne got up to help their kids. Then the server—she looked barely in her teens to Colt—invited him to sit at the table of his choice.

"Or did you want to join your friends?"

"Sure," said Cheyenne, at the same time as Leah said, "I don't think so."

Colt smiled away the awkward moment. "I'll have that table by the window, thanks." Once settled, he ordered coffee and pancakes and eggs, and tried to focus on the view out to the street. Instead, his gaze was drawn back to the family tableau. Leah and Cheyenne had finished helping their children and were now eating meals of their own.

He watched Leah cut into a stack of buttermilk pancakes, and transfer a forkful into her mouth. At just that moment she glanced at him, too, and though she looked away quickly, the fast-rising blush on her face gave her away. No matter what she'd said last night, she still felt something for him.

The uneasy feeling in his gut lifted then, and his appetite returned. He wasn't going to give up. She was too important to him for that.

He waited until Leah and Cheyenne finished paying the check and were on their way out the door. Leaving his half-finished meal on his table, he hurried to catch Leah before she was gone.

"Why don't you and the kids come out to Thunder Ranch tomorrow?" he asked. "Sunday is a slow day and I'll have time to give Jill a riding lesson if she wants."

"Yes! Please, Mommy, say yes!"

He'd been smart enough to issue the invitation so

the kids would hear it. He could tell by Leah's frown that she didn't appreciate his tactics. But he was surprised when she nevertheless appeared to be considering his offer.

"I'll think about it," she said. "How about I call you later tonight?"

"Do that."

Colt knew he had a stupid grin on his face as he returned to his table. He didn't care.

LEAH SPENT MOST OF that day thinking about Colt and considering his invitation to visit Thunder Ranch on Sunday. She knew she needed to protect herself and her children from getting too attached to a man who had spent his entire adult life avoiding ties and responsibility.

On the other hand, the fact that he had abandoned his own son wasn't really her business, as long as she kept their friendship on a strictly platonic level.

But was that possible? After all, she was dealing with Colton Hart here, the kind of cowboy, as Cheyenne had all too correctly pointed out, mommas warned their daughters about.

But...he was also her friend. Had been her friend for years. And it was thanks to him that she had landed Thunder Ranch as a client. When she'd checked her messages last night, she'd had calls from three prospective clients—calls she would return first thing Monday morning. She needed to keep on good terms with all the Harts to make sure they gave her a good referral.

Oh, good heavens. She was thinking in circles, trying to justify saying yes, when she knew in her heart that spending time with Colt was dangerous...even with her children present. She had to say no. She just had to.

She dialed Colt's cell number.

"Hey, Leah."

Just the sound of his voice saying her name did a number on the sensitive skin at the back of her neck. And even though she was alone in her living room, she could feel the color rising in her cheeks.

She tapped into her most professional voice. "Yes, Colt, about your invitation…"

"Yeah, good news. I managed to borrow a pony for Jill to ride."

"Really?"

"A nice, gentle mount. Belongs to a friend of a friend. Wasn't much trouble to get out to the ranch, though she did balk a little when we were trailering her."

Oh, my lord. He'd gone to all that work to get a pony for Jill to ride. How could she back out now without sounding rude?

"Jill is going to be so excited."

"Yeah." His voice softened. "I was kind of counting on that."

"You're diabolical, you know that?"

"Desperate situations call for desperate measures. See you tomorrow, Leah."

THEIR DAY AT Thunder Ranch lived up to every expectation. Colt suggested they begin with the pony and Jill took to riding like a natural. Sarah, who had changed after church and come out to watch, remarked to Leah, "She has a lovely seat for one so young."

"She does, doesn't she?" Leah wasn't surprised, but she was concerned. Riding lessons were expensive. Later, if Jill remained passionate about the sport, she would want her own horse. And that would be *crazy* expensive.

Still, how could she discourage her daughter's natural interest in horses, when she, herself, had gained so much joy from riding?

Leah sighed, and hitched a foot on the bottom rung of the fence. Sarah gave her a knowing look. "You're worried about the money."

"I'm that transparent?"

She laughed. "I had four children of my own, and a hand in raising my brother's two, as well. Every time one of them came up with a new interest or hobby, we felt it in the household budget. But somehow you find the money to support your children's passions."

"Thank you. You're right. That was exactly what I needed to hear." She'd been keeping an eye on Davey, who was playing in the dirt with his cars, throughout all of this. But suddenly he abandoned his game and started purposefully toward the arena. Leah moved to block him. "If you want to watch your sister, come stand with me."

"Don't want to watch. Want to swim."

Sarah stepped in quickly with an offer to take him to the pool.

"That's so kind," Leah said, "but you're always helping me with the kids. Davey can wait until Jill is finished her lesson."

"But you don't understand. I enjoy this, Leah, I really do."

"Colt mentioned you've had some trouble with your heart…."

"A little angina. My doctor says I need to avoid stressful situations, which is one reason I'm so thankful you're taking over my accounting duties. Now that was a job that always raised my blood pressure." She smiled, and squeezed Leah's shoulder.

"I know how busy life is on a ranch," Leah sympathized. "I'm sure you get precious little time to relax. Why don't you leave Davey here with me, and take some time for yourself?"

"But spending time with your children, that's a pure joy for me, Leah. Besides I need grandmother training—my first grandchild is due in a few months."

Leah could see this was an argument she wouldn't win. "In that case, thank you. Do you want to go swimming with Mrs. Hart, Davey?"

"Yes. Want to go."

After Sarah had taken his hand and led him away, Leah turned back to the arena, but she couldn't stop mulling over Sarah's last comment.

Colt's mother thought Ace and Flynn's child was going to be her first grandchild. But really, that honor should have gone to Colt's son, Evan. What would Sarah think if she knew the truth?

Would Colt ever tell her?

Leah shielded the sun from her eyes and focused not on Jill now, but on Colt. He seemed to be having as much fun as her daughter. Her heart ached to see them together, the child she loved so dearly, and the man who could be so much more, if he'd only give himself a chance.

"Lunch by your pool is becoming a habit, Mrs. Hart. Maybe our family should start running a tab that you can deduct from my accounting fees."

Truly, Leah was feeling guilty. Sarah had prepared a variety of salads, as well as hot pulled pork and fresh-from-the-oven dinner rolls.

Jill had insisted on a quick swim after her riding lesson, and now she and Davey were both dripping wet, wrapped in towels and sitting in the sun as they munched the deliciously gooey sandwiches.

Sarah waved a hand, as if to shoo away Leah's comment. "Oh, don't think of it that way, dear. You're a friend of Colt's, not just a business associate. And as I told you earlier, your children are warming me up for grandmother duties."

Leah glanced at Colt, wondering if he thought about Evan when his mother made comments like that. But his expression was inscrutable.

"Great spread, Mom," he said as he layered more of the tangy pulled pork on his freshly buttered roll. "Say, did you find any good bucking stock for sale in the paper earlier?"

"Yes, but everyone wants too much money. We broke the bank when we bought Midnight and I'm afraid we're going to have to negotiate a much better deal with our next purchase."

"Ace and Mom got swept up in a bidding war with our old neighbor, Earl McKinley," Colt told Leah, punctuating the comment with a devilish smile that made him look ridiculously appealing.

Oh, Colt. Why do you have to be so darn likeable?

She had to smile back. "Well, obviously the Harts emerged victorious."

"We got the horse," Sarah said drily. "We're still not so sure it was much of a victory."

"Are you kidding?" Colt almost choked as he reacted to his mother's comment. "You may have paid top dollar, but Midnight is worth every penny. He is one hell of a horse."

"He *looks* good," Sarah conceded. "But we bought him to be a stud horse and Ace hasn't had any success breeding him in the barn. He's just too unpredictable and we can't risk injuring the mares. We *have* had some success letting him out in the pasture with the mares. But it's not as safe or as reliable that way."

"Midnight has too much energy," Colt insisted. "That's the problem. You've got to let him burn off some steam on the rodeo circuit."

"It'll be a cold day in hell when we let that horse rodeo." All of them turned to see Ace, who had walked around the back of the house and had obviously overheard part of the conversation.

Chapter Twelve

"I've told you before, Colt," Ace continued, "we have too much invested in that horse to risk him getting injured."

Colt didn't argue with his brother. He just crossed his arms over his chest and stared down at the ground. It was left to Sarah to smooth over the gap in the conversation.

"Back from your call already? I didn't even hear you drive up." Sarah rose from her seat, then looked at the sky. "Gosh, where did those clouds come from? Sit down, Ace, there's plenty of food. I'll get extra plates for you and Flynn."

"Flynn was tired so I dropped her off at home." He leaned over the pulled pork and inhaled deeply. "But I won't say no to your offer."

"Good decision," Leah said. "It's delicious."

"Hey there, Leah. Excuse me, I didn't mean to ignore you. My brother knows how to yank my chain, I'm afraid."

"Isn't that what younger siblings are for? Davey does a pretty good job with Jill, too."

Ace smiled at the kids and their barbecue-sauce-smeared faces. "Looks like you guys have been enjoying my mom's pulled pork."

Leah laughed. "I was waiting for them to finish before I mopped them up."

"I rode a horse," Jill announced proudly, not at all self-conscious about her sticky face. "Colt teached me. He's Mommy's friend."

Ace blinked, but was quick to reply. "Well, you're learning from the best, sweetheart. If there's one thing my brother can do, it's ride horses."

While the comment was worded as a compliment, Ace's tone held the hint of a barb. Leah shot a discreet look in Colt's direction. He was looking down at his empty plate, his expression somewhat deflated. In a ranching family, skill with horses and the rodeo ought to be highly admired, and yet that didn't seem to be the case with Colt.

She couldn't understand why.

Finished with her meal, she cleared plates, then wiped Jill's and Davey's faces. The sky was considerably darker now as clouds continued to pile in from the mountains. The temperature had dropped several degrees, too, and Leah pulled warm sweatshirts over the kids' dry bathing suits. "We'll go home to shower and change," she told them, knowing they were going to protest.

But it was Ace who voiced the first objection. "Maybe you should wait a bit. I saw some serious thunderclouds out to the west when I was driving home. We're about to get hit with a storm, maybe even some hail."

And no sooner had he said that than the first drop fell.

"It's probably just a shower," Leah said. Sarah Hart had been so gracious, but she didn't want to outstay their welcome.

"Better not take the chance." Colt plucked up Davey

with one hand and the platter of pork with the other. "We can check the weather report from inside."

Since when did Colt call the shots for her and the children? Leah could tell that even Ace was a little taken aback by his brother's authoritative manner. But just then a loud crack of thunder had both kids shrieking. As if it had been a signal from a conductor, the sprinkles of raindrops turned into a torrent.

Suddenly everyone was rushing. Leah grabbed Jill and the bag with their clothes and towels, while Ace lowered the patio umbrella and packed up the rest of the food. Less than a minute later they were all inside the Harts' family room, damp and a little breathless. They'd no sooner shut the door behind them, than a second jolt of thunder shook through the house.

"Scawey." Davey reached for Leah to pick him up, but Jill turned to Colt.

"Are we safe in the house?"

"You bet we are, half-pint."

The confidence in his voice, even more than his words, seemed to reassure the children. As a distraction, Leah pulled a puzzle out from her bag—this was one of those times she was glad that she was always prepared—and scattered the pieces on the big coffee table near the river-rock fireplace. Both of her kids enjoyed puzzles, and they flocked to it.

Ace had gone to the barn to check on the livestock. Sarah was running around the house closing windows. That left Leah and Colt awkwardly avoiding one another's gazes.

Finally, he said, "I'll turn on the radio. See if we can find a weather report."

The great room opened right onto the kitchen, and that was where Colt headed. She followed him to the island, where she pulled up a stool and admired the stained cherry cabinets and limestone backsplash.

One day she'd love to have a house like this. Spacious, yet cozy, it was the sort of home that immediately made you feel comfortable. But owning a place like this was just a dream. As a single mother she'd be lucky if she could afford to buy, rather than just rent, the house she and the kids currently lived in.

Colt tuned the radio to a local station, which almost immediately broadcast an emergency weather bulletin. Sarah emerged from the hallway in time to hear it, too.

"The National Weather Service in Billings has issued a flash flood warning for Musselshell County—"

"Mom! Davey keeps taking the puzzle pieces away from me."

"Jill, hush, please. We're listening to something important."

Hearing the urgency in her mother's voice, Jill left the puzzle and came into the kitchen, with Davey tagging right behind her.

Leah had moved in front of the radio, as had Colt and his mother. All three of them listened intently as the broadcast continued.

"…reported water rising on the Musselshell River and approaching houses in Roundup—"

"Roundup, Mommy?" Jill pressed in closer. "That's where we live."

Leah shushed her, again, hardly noticing when Colt leaned over to pick up both kids, one in each arm. He seemed to be whispering something to them, but she just frowned and pressed in closer to the radio.

"Doppler radar indicates that another band of heavy rainfall is developing and moving over Musselshell County, producing rainfall rates up to one inch per

hour. Enhanced rainfall rates will likely cause flash flooding along the river bank in low-lying areas of Roundup. Residents should take immediate precautions to protect life and property—"

"Oh, my lord."

Immediately she thought about the smell in her basement. The house had flooded before and now it looked like it was about to happen again. Would it stop in the basement? Or would her entire home be submerged? Everything she and her children owned in the world was in that house. Everything.

"AT LEAST YOU KNOW your kids are safe and that's the main thing." Colt was driving his truck back to Roundup with Leah anxiously strapped into the passenger seat staring out at the wet, gray countryside.

"I wouldn't expect such sage advice from you. But you're right."

She'd neatly put him in his place but Colt could handle it. They were the only words she'd uttered since they'd turned off the radio and he was worried about her. Her face had gone so pale and her eyes seemed to be focused on some hidden, interior space that he had no access to.

His mother had suggested they wait out the storm before heading to town.

When Leah had shaken her head, Colt offered to drive, at which point his mother insisted that the children be left behind with her.

"Your mother is so kind," she said now, in a quiet voice he could hardly hear above the pounding of the rain against the cab roof. "Seems like I'm always thanking her for one thing or another."

"You know it's like a code in these parts. We all

help out our neighbors. Besides, she likes you, Leah. I can tell." A few times he'd noticed his mom glancing from him to Leah, then back again. He knew what she was hoping.

Sarah Hart was a smart woman and she'd picked up on the feelings between him and Leah. If only he was a different kind of man. A better kind of man...

He'd reached the end of Thunder Road. Colt checked for traffic, hoping no one was foolish enough to be driving without headlights in this pounding rain. Once he was on the highway, it seemed like the rain started coming down even harder. The windshield wipers couldn't go any faster, and he could barely see the road ahead. Still, he drove as fast as he dared, knowing that time was of the essence.

Ten minutes later they were on Timberline Drive. A group of men and women were down by the river, trying to create a sandbag barrier between the water and the town, but the bank had already risen to the footings of Leah's house. Fortunately the street had a couple feet elevation over the house, so Colt was able to drive almost up to the front door.

He stepped out into the drenching rain and met Leah on the lawn. A man covered in a black slicker and knee-high boots came up to talk to them. "You guys live here?" He pointed at Leah's house.

"I do," Leah said, her voice trembling. Colt put an arm around her shoulders and wish he could give her some of his strength to help her through this.

It was a frightening sight, for sure. The river was lapping up the backyard, muddy and roiling with debris.

"We already helped your neighbors evacuate," the man shouted, above the roar of the storm. "We'll be glad to give you a hand, too."

Leah seemed frozen in place, staring at her house. Colt's mother had lent her one of Dinah's old rain slickers, but she hadn't put up the hood and her hair and face were soaking wet. Gently Colt lifted the hood into place, then turned her so she would look at him.

"Wait in the cab. There are lots of people. This won't take long."

Leah shook her head. "I have to help."

She was soaking wet, probably in shock, too. But he could tell by the set of her jaw he wasn't going to win this one. If he could get her inside the house, out of the rain, maybe she'd be content with just giving instructions.

Of course she wasn't. She insisted on getting right in the action, tossing clothing, toys and kitchen supplies haphazardly into boxes and suitcases, then lugging them out to the truck. Someone had a tarp, and they tried to protect Leah's belongings from the rain as much as possible.

Amazingly, it took only thirty minutes to empty out the house, which was lucky. The river had crept up over the foundation—and it was only a matter of time before the road was washed out, too.

"We have to go, Leah." They'd thanked the volunteers who were already moving up to the next street, where sandbagging efforts were hoping to contain the river from reaching the next level of homes. Colt would have been pitching in, too, but he couldn't leave Leah.

She was shivering now, standing by his truck and looking forlornly at the jumbled mess in the back. The tarp was offering minimal protection as it flapped in the wind, despite Colt's efforts to tie it securely.

"Where should we take this?" he asked. "To your mother's?"

"I don't know."

He could see how hard she was fighting not to cry. He knew she and her mother had had a disagreement. Maybe Leah wasn't ready to face her, yet.

"Then we'll take it back to Thunder Ranch. Mom has lots of room in the basement. Our property sits nice and dry on high land."

"I can't do that, either. It's too much."

"Leah." He gave her shoulders a little shake. "We have to get this stuff out of the rain soon, or we might as well have left it in the house. Don't be too proud to accept help. Just tell me where to go—your mother's? Or Thunder Ranch?"

All he could see was her profile as she tilted her head away from him. Her face was soaking wet again— whether from rain or tears, he couldn't tell. Probably both.

"I don't know," she said, again. "I have no idea what to do." With that, she broke completely from his grasp and climbed back into the passenger seat of his truck.

LEAH SAT IN THE TRUCK, shivering, barely noticing when Colt joined her. He started the truck, drove to the top of the road, then pulled over. She supposed he was waiting for her to make a decision. He might be waiting a long time.

What else could go wrong? Leah felt as if the rain had washed away every bit of her hope and optimism. The new home she'd worked so hard to build for her children—gone. They'd been lucky to salvage their belongings, but even that was an empty victory. Where was she supposed to put the children's beds, their toys, all of their clothing?

"The engine's finally warm. We'll get some heat

now." Colt turned the truck's heater up to high and hot air blasted over Leah's chilled body. "Are you okay?"

"Sure." What else could she say? Colt had done so much to help her, she couldn't tell him how awful she felt. She knew she ought to be grateful that she and the children were safe and, of course, she was, but that didn't make their losses any less significant.

Two months ago she'd moved her children out of the house where they'd been born.

Now they were homeless again.

She felt a warm hand on her head. She turned to see Colt watching her, the look in his eyes full of tender concern. He stroked her head one more time, then reached for her hand and gave her a squeeze.

"You're going to be okay, Leah Stockton. You're a strong woman and you have lots of people who care about you."

"Thanks, Colt." That was just what she'd needed to hear. She knew she had people who cared, and her mother, for all their differences, was one of them.

She reached inside her jacket pocket for her phone. To her surprise she saw five missed calls, all from her mom. The storm had been so loud, she hadn't heard any of them.

She hit the call button and her mom answered within two seconds.

"Leah? Are you and the kids okay?"

"Yes, Mom, we're fine."

"I heard there was flooding in your area."

"Yes. We just finished getting our stuff out. Colt and a bunch of neighbors helped me."

"Oh, dear. This is so terrible."

Leah couldn't dispute that.

"Don't you wonder, honey, if it isn't a sign? Nothing's

gone right since you left Jackson. Maybe later tonight
you could call him. Just to talk. I assume you and the
kids will be staying with me again?"

For a minute Leah couldn't say a word. Just when
she needed a kind word, there it was, a stab in the heart.
To be fair, she didn't think her mom meant to hurt her.
Still, she couldn't deal with this now.

She could tell Colt had heard every word her mother
had said. He was quietly watching for her reaction and
she covered the phone so her mother wouldn't hear.

"Is your offer still open?" she asked him.

"It is."

She uncovered the phone. "Mom, the house didn't
flood because I left Jackson. It flooded because we've
had too much rain. And no—the kids and I won't be
staying with you. We'll be at Thunder Ranch until I
find us a new home."

"YOU MADE THE right decision," Colt said. "The suite
where Ace used to live is empty. Lots of room there
for you and the kids."

"But it's connected to the main house, right? So we'll
need to ask your mother."

"A mere technicality."

That wasn't the point. Leah had no doubt that Sarah
would take them in. But it seemed too much to ask.
Sarah was her employer, not her family.

"Is there any place else? A cabin somewhere? We
don't need anything fancy."

"Well, you could take my trailer and I could move
into the suite. It would be a definite step up for me, but
pretty cramped for you and the kids."

"We wouldn't care. As long as you don't mind?"

"Hell no. Like I said, it's a good deal for me. But you

may want to check out my trailer before you give up dibs on Ace's suite."

By the time they returned to the ranch, the rain had stopped and sunlight filtered through the dissipating clouds. Colt ran his plan by Sarah, who was in the process of cooking a roast beef for Sunday dinner while the children—whom Sarah had helped shower and change—were now watching a movie in the adjoining great room. Ace and Flynn were expected to join them for the meal, as well as Sarah's brother, Joshua, and both of his sons.

"I'm so sorry about your house, Leah." Hands wet from peeling potatoes, Sarah used the back of her wrist to push back a strand of hair that had fallen in her eyes. "You and the children are very welcome at Thunder Ranch—as you can see we have loads of room. Please stay wherever you'll be most comfortable. Colt's camper is pretty tiny. Are you sure you wouldn't be happier in Ace's old suite? There's a big bed for you and we could set up cots for the children."

"We'll be fine in the camper. Thank you so much for taking us in." Sarah had done so much for her today. With her heart condition, it just wasn't right. Leah longed for a shower and a change of clothes. Instead she reached for the peeler. "Why don't you rest for a few minutes. I can handle this."

Sarah ceded the job gratefully. "I'm not going to say no to that. Peel the entire bag, please, Leah. My boys are big eaters."

LEAH WAS WORRIED that the commotion of a Hart family Sunday dinner might be too much for her children, but as the evening progressed it was Leah who felt overwhelmed. It had been a long, hard day and not only had she chipped in to help Sarah prepare the meal, but now she also had to try and keep all the new family members straight.

First to arrive was Sarah's brother and his two sons. Colt commissioned them to help unload her belongings from the back of his truck into the basement. When they were finished, all four men trouped into the house, making the spacious home feel suddenly much smaller.

Joshua Adams was a ruggedly handsome man, much taller than his sister. As soon as he stepped into the kitchen, Sarah offered him a beer and the carving knife, both of which he seemed very comfortable accepting.

"I knew your father," he told Leah. "A good man. I was sorry to hear that your mother sold the farm after he passed. That was a nice piece of land."

"Yes, it was. But Mom is happier in town."

Colt handed her another two beers and asked her to pass them along to his cousins. Duke seemed to be the quieter of the twins. He'd brought his dog Zorro with him, a beautifully gentle German shepherd who put up with all the attention Davey and Jill immediately lavished on him.

"Sorry about your break-in, Aunt Sarah." Duke took a sip from his beer, as he kept an eye on Zorro and the kids. "We're going to do all we can to find the thieves and recover your belongings."

"Thank you, Duke. You know the saddle is what I care about most."

"The law is on it, Aunt Sarah." Beau gave his brother a supportive slap on the shoulder before offering a hand to Leah. "Don't believe we've had the pleasure—?"

No sooner had Colt finished with the introduction, than Ace and Flynn arrived and a new round of hellos were made, and more drinks were handed out. Leah had just found a quiet moment to pour her children glasses of milk, when Sarah announced that dinner was served.

The flash flood in Roundup was the first subject of interest at the table and, not wanting to alarm the children, Leah did her best to make the miserable events of that afternoon sound like an exciting adventure. It took a lot of energy, though—energy she was about to run out of—and she was glad when the topic was finally exhausted and talk turned to the next rodeo on the family's schedule, the Yellowstone Roundup in Gardiner.

"We're booked up for that one," Sarah said. "All available bulls and bucking stock. I hope everyone is planning on helping?"

A chorus of affirmations went around the table, then Colt added, "Might be the perfect time to get Midnight back in the arena."

Ace gave his brother a dirty look. "You don't give up, do you?"

"Your opinion isn't the only one that matters around here. What about the rest of the family—shouldn't we hear what they think?"

"You talking about entering Midnight Express in the rodeo?" Uncle Joshua asked. "Kinda risky, isn't it? What if he gets hurt?"

"My point, exactly," Ace said.

"But think of the extra money," Beau countered. "Not to mention the prestige. Midnight is the kind of horse a cowboy waits his whole career to get a chance on."

Both Ace and Colt tried to speak then, with the result that neither one of them could be understood. From the head of the table, Sarah rapped her knife against her water glass. The ringing tone brought the conversation to a swift halt.

"Enough arguing, please. With so many of us gathered together today I think it's appropriate that we drink a toast to those who are missing…Dinah and, of course, Tuf." She raised her glass. "May they both return safely home, soon."

The toast was echoed around the table. And then Leah, who had thought the day really couldn't hold any more surprises, watched in openmouthed mortification as Jill raised her half-full milk glass to the table.

"To my daddy," she said. "He's coming home soon, too."

Chapter Thirteen

By the time dinner was over, Jill and Davey were practically asleep in their chairs. Flynn insisted Leah leave the dishes. "Ace and I will do them. You've had a long day."

Truer words had never been spoken. But Leah eyed Flynn's pregnant belly doubtfully. "Are you sure?"

Flynn laughed. "I have so much energy these days, it's crazy. And Ace, well, there's nothing he enjoys more than helping me in the kitchen."

She flung a dishcloth in her husband's direction and he caught it with one hand. "Darlin', I think it's another room in the house where I have my real expertise."

Leah gave Flynn a grateful hug, said her thanks to Sarah and her farewells to the others, then, with Colt's help, ushered her children outside.

In the aftermath of the storm, the evening air was warm and muggy. Colt led the way to his trailer, carrying a suitcase in one hand and holding onto Jill with the other. As soon as Leah saw the twenty-two-foot Airstream that was to become their temporary home, she had second thoughts about the feasibility of their plan. Colt had warned her it was small, but gosh…it sure looked tiny.

The kids squealed with delight, though, and would have immediately dashed inside if she hadn't stopped them.

"Just wait a sec, okay, until I figure out how we're going to do this."

Colt opened the side door for her and she stuck her head inside. To the right was the bathroom. Ahead was a closet and a galley kitchen, with a little vase containing wildflowers on the counter. *When had Colt found time to do that?* A sofa, which had already been converted to a double bed, with sheets, pillows and a coverlet was at the other end of the trailer, and a second converted bed faced the kitchen.

"Wow. Not an inch is wasted in here, is it?" She was touched by Colt's efforts to make his humble home comfortable and welcoming.

"Changed your mind?"

It would be like camping for a few weeks. They could do this. "Nope. We're all in. Kids, take off your shoes and leave them on the steps. This is going to be fun."

IT COULD HAVE GONE either way. The kids were so thrilled with the compact trailer they might have giggled and played for hours before settling down. But the day of sun and rain, play and new experiences eventually won out and they dropped off in exhausted sleep fifteen minutes after squirming into their pj's.

Finally Leah had time to decompress. She brushed her hair and put it in a single French braid running down her back. Then she washed and changed into an old pair of gym shorts and a tank top. Not wanting to turn on any lights outside the bathroom, she used a mini book light and tried to lose herself in her novel.

But, face it. Too much had happened in her life today for her to focus on a fictional woman's problems.

Plus, she was antsy. She needed a little room and some fresh air. She decided to turn off the air-conditioning and open the windows in the trailer, so she would hear if either of the kids woke up. Then she slipped on her boots and stepped outside.

Colt's trailer sat on a bluff, looking out over an expanse of grazing land with the Bull Mountains profiled in the distance. Though it was nine o'clock, the sun had just slipped behind the mountains, casting the wispy clouds in a rosy, amber glow.

A wooden picnic table was positioned about twenty feet from the trailer and she sat on the table, with her feet planted on the bench, to watch the show.

After a few minutes, she heard rustling from the woods that divided the main house from the trailer. Seconds later, Colt emerged from the path.

He was wearing a fresh pair of jeans and a white T-shirt. His damp hair was already curling up around his ears. "Pretty sunset, huh?"

"It's very peaceful out here." She felt a buzz of awareness as he sat next to her on the table, close enough that she could smell the shampoo he'd used on his hair.

He'd shaved, too, she noticed.

She ran a hand down her bare calves. Too bad she hadn't. Then she laughed silently at herself. As if it mattered. What a strange thing to even think about on a day like today.

"Peaceful is good, right?"

"Peaceful is very good."

"Kids settle all right?"

"Surprisingly so."

They were silent for a few beats, then Colt laughed. "That was quite the toast your daughter made at dinner."

Leah covered her face with her hands then sighed.

"These are the kinds of mind games my mother plays with my children. The poor things are so confused now."

"I guess it's only natural they want their mom and dad to be together."

"Yes." It was easy to feel guilty about that. But feeling guilty didn't solve anything. "It's never going to happen, though."

"You're sure?"

"Positive."

The colors on the western horizon were blazing now—a beautiful harmony of golds and peaches, roses and violets. Leah turned to face the cowboy beside her. His skin glowed with reflected rays from the sunset. She could even see the colors in his eyes.

"Leah—" He swallowed. "I can't stop wanting you."

She felt the meaning of his words in every nerve and every cell of her being. Being this close to him—it was torture. He had to know she felt the same way.

He took hold of the braid running down her back, and tugged gently, moving her closer to him.

And then they were kissing again. Why did this keep happening? No matter how many resolutions they made, it always came back to this. He wanted her, and she, Lord help her, wanted him.

She loved the feel and taste of his lips. A tender exploring kiss soon became possessive, then demanding. She couldn't resist reaching out to feel the strength of his shoulders and his back, but even as she allowed herself that much luxury she knew she wanted more, so much more this time.

His hands burned through the thin cotton of her tank top, as he caressed her torso, moving up to brush over her breasts, then back down to slide under her baggy gym shorts.

"You're so damn sexy, Leah. Every sweet inch of you."

If this was wrong, why did it feel so darn good? Colt laid her gently back onto the picnic table, then sank down beside her. He kissed her on the lips again, then on her neck, and her collarbone. She shivered as he laid further claim to her bare shoulder, then her belly, and finally, tugging up on her tank top, her breasts.

Don't stop. Don't stop. Her body pleaded, begged, for more. When his hands settled at her hips, she raised them from the table, letting him shimmy down the shorts, so he could touch and fondle—*sweet heaven, yes*—some more.

Oh, he was good, so very, very good. And Leah was thankful for the darkness that was settling over them now, the darkness that made it possible for her world to shrink to this moment, and these feelings, and this man.

She tried to fight the rising tidal wave, but Colt was relentless. He pushed her over and she muffled her screams, pressing her arm against her mouth as her body throbbed with the pleasure that he had given her.

"Yes, darling," he encouraged her, coming up to cradle her in his arms. "My beautiful Leah."

She nuzzled his neck, pressing her body urgently into his. "Cowboy, your talents do not lie only in the rodeo arena…."

His teeth flashed in the dark as he smiled at her. "It's about time you realized that."

Something was wrong here. He'd become far too relaxed.

"Um, Colt?" She'd lost her boots at some point. Now she wrapped her top leg—her *unshaven* leg—over his thigh. He was still wearing his jeans, for heaven's sake. Hadn't even undone the top button of his shirt! "Am I missing something? I thought we were going to—" she paused to kiss him "—continue?"

He smoothed a hand down her torso, gently repositioning her top, then pulled her shorts back into position. "Our first time is not going to be on a picnic table."

"Oh, really?" A little of the pleasure haze was beginning to lift. "And what if this was it—your only chance." She pushed back on his chest, creating a space of several inches between them.

He kissed her nose anyway. "It won't be."

"You're awfully sure of yourself. I never should have said that thing about you having talents other than the rodeo." She unhitched his arm from her waist and pushed up into a sitting position.

He just propped his head up with his arm and gave her another flash of his white teeth.

"You look far too pleased with yourself right now." She found her boots on the ground and shoved her feet back into them. In a flash, Colt was off the table, standing next to her.

"I am pleased. But maybe not for the reason you think."

The flirting tone was gone. Colton Hart actually sounded serious, for a change.

"Oh?"

"I figured out something today, Leah."

"What—don't rent property in flood zones?"

He grasped her shoulders. "Not to be cruel, but I already knew that, darling. No, I figured out something a lot more important."

She planted her hands on her hips. "Well? Going to clue me in?"

He ran a finger along her cheek, his touch so gentle her heart ached. "Not quite yet. But eventually."

Colt was too wired to go to sleep. Having Leah and her kids at the Hart Sunday dinner had been a mind-blowing experience for him. They'd fit in so well. It was like they already belonged.

The credit went to Leah. She'd raised two awesome kids. And the way she'd stepped up to the plate in the kitchen—that had been awesome, too.

Given the day she'd had, everyone would have understood if she'd taken a little time to have a shower, rest and change for dinner. But she'd just washed her hands in the kitchen sink and gone straight to work. He knew his mother had been impressed.

And so was he.

He'd dated a lot of women who went all out with their makeup and hair and their designer Western wear. But when it came to looking for a life-partner, he'd pick Leah over them any day.

But then he'd always known that Leah was amazing. The big question was—did he deserve her?

Any objective observer would say the answer was no. But maybe it wasn't too late for him. Maybe he could change—become a better man.

For too many years he'd let himself be buffeted by circumstances and fate. In particular, he'd allowed a twelve-year-old legal document to define his life.

And that was wrong.

Figure out what you don't do well—and don't do it.

It was time he modified Uncle Josh's saying, Colt figured. *Figure out what you really want—then earn it.*

He would start tomorrow.

COLT WOKE BEFORE dawn, dressed in his work clothes and went out to start the morning chores. After an hour of pitching hay and mucking stalls, he spotted his mother by Midnight's paddock.

"Mom?" He removed his gloves and set them on a fence post. "Can I talk to you about something?"

She shaded her eyes against the rising sun. "If this is about letting Midnight rodeo, can we please discuss it later? I hate to spoil a beautiful morning with an old argument."

"It's not about that." Though he did intend to eventually get his way on that point, he had other matters to settle with his mother. "Ace has been after me to take on more responsibility at the ranch for a long time."

"Well, you do spend more time on the rodeo circuit than anyone else—and not always helping with the bucking stock, either."

He knew it was true. He often let his own rodeoing ambitions lead him further astray than the local rodeos they serviced with their broncs and bulls. He needed the money. But personal glory came along with the package. "Rodeo is what I do. It's what I'm good at. Plus, it's not the easiest thing in the world for me to take orders from Ace. He's my brother and I love him. But— He's just so damn perfect. I can't live up to that. I've never been able to."

His mom laid a hand on his arm. "He's an amazing man, your brother. But you have your own strengths. I know your father never let you know how proud he was of your abilities. But let me tell you, he bragged enough to our friends about you."

That was news to him. He almost didn't believe it. But his mother was too honest to lie.

"What I'm trying to say, Mom, is that I'd like my own area of responsibility at Thunder Ranch."

His mom tilted her head. "What are you thinking?"

"Up until now, you and Ace have been managing the bucking stock operation between the two of you. What if I took over? You could spend more time with that new grandchild you're expecting. And Ace could devote more energy to his family and his vet practice."

Surprise and relief washed over his mother's face, followed immediately by skepticism. "How do you see this working?"

"Specifically?"

She nodded.

"Well, I'll book the rodeos and arrange transport and care of the livestock."

"You'll actually go to the rodeos, too? Not run off to do your own thing? I hate to sound harsh, Colt, but in the past—"

His mother raised a valid point. "It'll be different now. For the most part I'll limit my competing to the rodeos we're servicing. There is one catch, though— I'll need to draw a salary. Doesn't have to be much, but I have to compensate for the drop in my rodeo winnings somehow."

His mom studied his face. He knew she was wondering what he did with his money, since he obviously didn't live high on the hog. But she didn't ask questions, just nodded her acceptance.

"That's fair, Colt. As long as you also order feed and arrange vet and farrier services…" Sarah began to list the dozens of responsibilities that went with maintaining a string of bucking horses.

"Yup. All of that. Plus, I'd like a hand in building the operation." He took a deep breath. It was time to let his mother know what he'd been working on the past few months. "I've been talking to Brad Mackay from Stillwater. He's looking to get out of the business. We've had a few meetings already—one of them was the morning of Ace's wedding—and I've looked over his herd. There are half a dozen horses that would make a great addition to our string."

Colt could tell his mother was impressed. "I heard those rumors, too. Never bothered following up because word had it Brad had a pretty firm buyer lined up."

"That would be me. Brad's son and I go way back. And Brad's the kind of man who cares where his horses go."

"That sounds too good to be true. But, Colt...do you have any idea how much work you're signing up for?"

He looked straight into his mother's eyes. "Sure, I do."

"You'll have to sacrifice more than just your travel schedule. You'll also have less time to help Uncle Josh and Beau with the cattle."

That would be a real loss. Colt loved the time he spent working with the cattle, out on the land. "I'm not a kid anymore, Mom. I'm a man. And it's time I took on a man's set of responsibilities around here."

To his surprise, his mother's eyes filled with tears. She put her hand on his arm, then reached up to kiss his cheek.

"I never thought I'd hear those words from you, Colt. Oh, how I wish your father could have heard them, too."

COLT SHARED A brief breakfast with his mother, before she headed off to volunteer at Angie Barrington's animal rescue, something she did for the therapeutic benefits of working with needy animals. Lisa Marie, the woman Ace had hired to help with the housework, wasn't due for another hour. That gave him time to put the final, most difficult phase of his plan into action.

Using the address he knew by heart, he was able to find the Great Falls phone number. He punched the digits into his phone, then hit Call.

While he waited to see if anyone would pick up, he paced in front of the fireplace.

A woman answered, her voice immediately familiar to him. "Colt Hart? I can't believe you're phoning me after all these years."

He almost couldn't get out any words. "I—I figured my call wouldn't be welcome. You had things pretty well-organized by the time I heard from your lawyer."

There was a long pause. "That was twelve years ago. If you had any problems with my plan, you could have been in touch."

"What can I say? It's taken me a long time to grow up."

"Our son is almost a teenager."

Our son. The fact that she'd worded it that way gave him hope.

"Does he know about me?"

"I've always been truthful with Evan. About everything."

Colt pressed a fist to his forehead. God, he'd been such an idiot. Why had he waited so long? "Do you think he'd be willing to meet me?"

"I'll ask, but I'm pretty sure the answer will be yes. He's followed your career, Colt. He doesn't say much, but I can tell he's pretty proud."

Of what? Rodeo buckles and all-around cowboy trophies? Both seemed meaningless to Colt right now.

"I have an idea, Janet. Tell me what you think—"

Chapter Fourteen

When his call was over, Colt filled a thermos with coffee and made his way to the office. Leah and the kids were already there. She'd set them up with coloring books and toys on the floor, while she worked away at the accounting records.

She blushed when she saw him and if it hadn't been for Jill and Davey he wouldn't have been able to resist kissing her.

"How was the first night in the trailer?"

"Fun!" Jill said.

Davey echoed his sister, punctuating his comment with a clap of his chubby hands.

Colt grabbed two clean mugs from the shelf and poured out coffee for himself and Leah. "Is it okay, black?"

"If it's hot and has caffeine, I'll take it."

He leaned against the desk, peering down at the computer screen. The rows of numbers meant precious little to him.

"I've just been put in charge of the bucking horses at Thunder Ranch."

Leah looked impressed, just as he'd hoped.

"Now that I've been promoted to management, I

think it's time I learned to read financial reports. You up to giving me a lesson sometime?"

"I'll be glad to teach you a thing or two, Colton Hart."

No missing the teasing lilt to her words. God, he wished her kids weren't in the room with them right now. "I'll hold you to that. So...how did you find the bed last night?" He leaned closer and whispered, "Lonely?"

She pushed him back with a hand to his chest. "It was perfect, actually. We all slept really well," Leah admitted, as if she couldn't quite believe it.

"I hope you helped yourself to whatever food you could find for breakfast." He didn't stock much, but he kept essentials like bread, cereal and milk.

"We did. Fruit Loops, Colt. At your age?"

"I bet Davey and Jill didn't complain."

"You're right, they were pretty pleased. I plan to go to town to restock this afternoon. And while I'm there I'm going to see about hiring someone to come out and babysit for the rest of the week. I'd really like to finish this by Friday, if possible."

"Do you have other jobs lined up?"

"I hope so. I've had some calls and I've made a few appointments for next week. With any luck I'll land at least a couple of new clients."

She pulled her hair back into a makeshift ponytail, then let it fall around her shoulders. He loved that messy look. Made him think of last night on the picnic table...

As if reading his mind, she waved a pencil at him. "You aren't allowed to think that way when my children are present."

He feigned innocence. "Me? I just came in here to check the rodeo schedule."

To prove the point, he moved to the white board

where the next six weeks were all mapped out in red marker. Too bad Ace and his mother had already committed their string for the Yellowstone Roundup in Gardiner. The annual PRCA rodeo in Belt was on the exact same weekend.

He'd promised his mother he would travel with the bucking stock from now on, but he'd just have to start a few weeks later than planned. Ace would give him hell, but once he found out the reason, hopefully he'd understand.

"Why do you look so worried?"

Because my whole future is riding on this. Correction—*our* whole future.

"I'm not worried," he denied. "But if you and the kids are looking for something fun to do this weekend, I've heard it's going to be a real exciting year at the rodeo in Belt."

"You wouldn't happen to be registered, would you?"

"Steer wrestling and bull riding..."

Her eyes grew wide. "Now that would be something for the kids to see."

It would. But she was the one he wanted to impress. In more ways than one.

"I'll be going down on Friday night," he said. "It would be great to see you there on Sunday."

"I'll think about it."

"Think hard."

EVER SINCE HE'D helped her during the flash flood, there'd been something different about Colt. Leah would see him striding purposefully across the yard, talking animatedly to the hired hands, or exercising Midnight in his round pen. He had a new assuredness about him. Oh, he'd always been confident, but in a cocky way and this was different. Leah was afraid to hope, but the word that came to mind was *maturity*.

Was it possible that Colt Hart had finally decided there were some things in life worth getting serious about?

And was she crazy to think that she might be one of them?

She didn't see enough of him that week to test her theory. He put in long days at work, and so did she. She'd had a total of five calls in response to her ads so far, and had lined up several meetings with prospective clients for the afternoons when she wasn't working on the Thunder Ranch accounts.

Jill wanted to ask him for more riding lessons. Leah told her she had to be patient since Colt was very busy right now. Jill was also getting more curious about the relationship between her mother and Colt, and Leah had to field several of those questions, too. Gently she explained that after a divorce, mommies and daddies sometimes started dating other people—and yes, she and Colt were sort of at that stage. Davey listened to all of their conversations, but Leah had no idea how much of it he actually took in.

While in town on Monday, Leah went to speak with the young waitress Cheyenne had recommended. Jessica Crane was a bright eighteen-year-old, saving for college and needing more hours than Sierra could give her at the Number 1.

Jessica had her driver's license and use of her parents' car, which meant she could travel to and from the ranch on her own. She also had a lot of energy and a sweet way with the kids that quickly won their hearts—and Leah's.

Though, when it came to Jill and Davey, Colt was still the number one guy they wanted to hang out with.

"Next week," he'd promised Jill when she begged for another riding lesson. Leah had given Jill a calendar and every night they crossed off one of the days to help her understand when this lesson would happen.

Hopefully nothing would come up that would require Colt to cancel.

COLT ASKED HIS MOTHER to call a family meeting to discuss the changes that they'd agreed on. He meant to do this right, and that meant having everyone in the family on board. Above all, he hoped that Ace would be good with the new arrangement.

His older brother had been complaining for a long time about having too much work and responsibility at the ranch. But would he be willing to give up a share of the authority, as well? Ace had been calling the shots for a long time. Nothing he liked better, as far as Colt could tell, than bossing his siblings around.

Would he be ready to take a backseat in some areas?

Colt could tell that his mother had her reservations, too. She organized the meeting for Wednesday evening after dinner and Ace and Flynn were the first people she called, checking on Ace's schedule before she phoned the rest of the family. Joshua, Beau and Duke were good with Wednesday, and since Dinah was back in town, she was invited as well, even though she didn't have much involvement in the day-to-day operations of the ranch.

All in all, there were eight of them milling around the coffee and homemade cookies that Sarah had set out on the kitchen table. Only Tuf was missing. His youngest brother still hadn't returned home, and all of them were wondering what it was he didn't want to tell them.

Because there had to be some reason he was avoiding his home and his family now that he was finally out of the marines.

"Help yourself to coffee everyone. It's decaf. And Lisa Marie made the cookies fresh today."

Colt made a point of saying hello to his sister, whom he hadn't seen since Ace's wedding day. She barely met his eyes when she said hello back. She and Ace had always been close, and he suspected she was still holding a grudge against him for missing the ceremony.

"Just for the record—" he went to stand beside her as she poured coffee from the carafe into her mug "—the reason I was late for the wedding was because I had a meeting with Brad Mackay. He's planning to retire this fall and he's agreed to sell us six of their top-ranked bucking horses."

"I don't care if he agreed to sell you the entire business. You missed your brother's wedding." She grabbed a cookie and took a big bite, as if to signify there was nothing else to say.

Colt knew there was no point explaining that the meeting had been set up before Ace told him about the wedding. The fact was, he *could* have rescheduled the meeting. In fact *should* have done so.

"Yeah, I blew it, big-time." Especially since Tuf hadn't been there, either, which meant Ace had been missing both of his brothers. Colt reached for a cookie, too, and absentmindedly took a bite. Ace was standing by the fireplace, talking to their mother. Colt hoped Sarah was softening him up for the news to come. He needed his brother to be okay with the new arrangement. There were already too many areas of contention between them.

Most of them his fault, Colt conceded. That was something else he had to set right. And tonight he was taking the first step.

"If everyone is ready, let's get this family meeting started," Sarah announced. "Why don't we sit around the table and get comfortable."

It didn't take long for everyone to settle down as she'd requested. No one wanted this meeting to go on too late—they all had jobs and lots of work waiting for them in the morning.

Without preamble, Sarah made the announcement that Colt was taking over responsibility for the bucking horse side of the business. "Joshua and Beau will continue managing the cattle and the bulls. And Ace will be free to concentrate on his veterinary practice and the breeding program. Still, everyone will be expected to pitch in as needed, the way we've always done."

She set her hands flat on the table. "Questions?"

There was a long moment of silence. Colt realized he wasn't the only one looking at Ace. Beside him, Flynn had a happy smile. No big surprise there. Flynn had turned Ace's proposals down numerous times because she thought he was a workaholic unable to fully commit to a wife and a baby.

Now Ace would have more time for both. But how would he feel about that?

The tension in the room rose as Ace set his coffee mug down loudly on the table, and turned to face Colt. "About damn time," he finally said.

Relief hit Colt with the same power as the eight-second timer in the rodeo ring. Suddenly he could breathe again. And smile. Maybe this was going to work out even better than he'd thought.

THE TRUCE BETWEEN the brothers didn't last long, however. In fact, it was put to the test on Thursday afternoon, when Colt spotted Ace and his mother outside Midnight's paddock and went to talk to them.

"How's he doing?" Colt asked his brother, referring to the stallion.

"Gracie said he's been hard to handle this week. It's not the progress I was hoping for. I have a bunch of mares we want to pasture breed next week. I don't want to risk any injuries, though. Maybe I should call it off."

"It's your decision, Ace," Sarah said.

"I wouldn't cancel if I was you." They'd talked all nicey-nicey during the family meeting on Wednesday, but Colt figured the time had come to face the elephant in the room. "Breeding season is almost over. This might be one of your last opportunities to collect some stud fees for this calendar year."

"That's true, but if Midnight hurts one of the mares, the consequences won't be good."

"He won't hurt them if he gets the chance to blow off some steam at the rodeo this weekend."

Ace's features tightened with anger. "Forget it. Not going to happen."

"You're forgetting something here. *I'm* in charge of the bucking stock program now."

Ace squared off against Colt. "And *I'm* in charge of the breeding program. We bought Midnight to be a stud. That makes me the boss of what happens with him."

"*You* may have decided Midnight should be a full-time stud. But what about what Midnight wants? I'm telling you that stallion needs some kick-ass action. He grew up on it. Was bred for it. And he'll keep on raising hell until he gets it."

His brother stepped forward, using his extra few

inches of height to unfair advantage. "Just because that's how your mind works doesn't mean—"

"What the hell? You want to make this personal?" Colt might not be as tall as Ace, but he knew if he could wrestle a three-hundred-pound steer to the ground, he could give Ace a good fight. They hadn't done this in years, but damn it, it sure seemed as if that's what Ace was looking for....

"Boys!" Sarah stepped between her sons, looking appalled. "I'm going to have to fire you both if I ever see you try to handle your differences this way again."

She glared at Ace. "You don't use intimidation tactics with anyone else. Why with Colt?"

The fight went right out of Ace then. He rubbed a hand over his chin, as he took a moment to compose himself. "You're right, Mom. I apologize." He stuck out his hand and Colt shook it.

"Me, too," he said.

"That's better. I expect you boys to resolve your differences like adults from here on in."

Colt really felt ashamed now. The last thing their mom needed with her angina was for them to act like schoolyard thugs. "I'm sorry, too, Mom, but I'm not sure where to go from here. Ace has his mind set one way, and mine is equally set in the other."

Sarah chuckled. "Well, at least you boys aren't wishy-washy." She set her hands on her hips and studied each of her son's faces in turn. Then she sighed. "Since you two are locked down, I guess as the ranch owner, I'll have to cast the deciding vote."

Colt nodded, as did Ace. What their mother had said was absolutely right. Ultimately no one had a bigger stake in this place than she did.

"I have to admit that, like Ace, I'm worried about

risking injury to Midnight. That horse cost us so much money, sometimes I still wake up in a cold sweat over it."

Oh, crap. Colt struggled to keep the disappointment out of his expression as he waited for his mother to finish. He should have known she'd side with Ace.

"But despite my concerns," Sarah continued, "I'm going to vote with Colt on this one. We try one rodeo. Just one. If Midnight isn't injured, if he settles down with the mares, then we'll talk about letting him do more."

FRIDAY MORNING, Colt cornered Ace in his office before he'd left on any calls. His brother was sitting at the desk jabbing at the keyboard attached to an archaic computer. Two cardboard boxes were stacked next to the small refrigerator in the corner, and Colt sat on them.

"Bet you're looking forward to moving someplace bigger soon." The plan was to eventually relocate Ace's vet practice to the McKinley ranch, where he and Flynn lived. But until Midnight had completely settled, Ace was staying put.

"I'd also like a computer that didn't take longer to think than I do." Ace typed for a minute longer, then looked up. "So? Something on your mind?"

Colt looked down at his dusty, well-worn boots. "I need a favor."

"You mean another one?"

If Ace needed him to eat dirt, he'd eat dirt. "Okay, then, yes. Another one."

"I'm listening."

"I managed to book Midnight in at Belt for the weekend. I'd like you to come with me."

"Belt? But I thought it was the Roundup in Gardiner

this weekend? Flynn and I were both planning to attend that one. I promised her a side trip to Yellowstone after."

"Well. That's where the rest of the stock is going. But Midnight's going to Belt. And so am I."

"How long have you been registered?"

Colt saw the doubt in his brother's eyes. He thought he was up to his old tricks, doing his own thing, not being a team player. "I registered Midnight and myself yesterday afternoon. It's a small, local rodeo, won't be too much pressure."

Colt had other reasons for picking Belt. But he couldn't tell his brother yet.

"Yeah, it's probably a good idea not to start Midnight with something too big. But what do you need me for? Gracie's handled that horse more than any of us."

"True, but her kids have finals next week and she needs to keep an eye on them this weekend and make sure they study. Besides, I need a hazer."

"You're entered in steer wrestling?"

"Yup. Bull riding, too."

Ace stared at him for a good long minute. Colt guessed he was thinking the same thing he was. If Midnight did happen to get injured at the rodeo, it would be good to have his vet along.

"Okay, I'll break the news to Flynn."

"Thanks. I owe you one."

"Two," Ace reminded him.

Chapter Fifteen

If she hadn't told the kids about the rodeo, Leah probably would have changed her mind about going on Sunday. She'd hardly seen Colt all week. She tried to tell herself that was because of his new responsibilities, but she couldn't help thinking that those new responsibilities might change more than she'd bargained for.

At least Colt had said goodbye to her before he and Ace left on Friday morning, with Midnight in tow.

Trailering the stallion had been the usual challenge and Leah hoped things would go okay at the rodeo. She'd heard from Gracie about the big debate between the two brothers, and how Sarah herself had had to step in to resolve matters.

Leah thought it was brave of Sarah to have sided with Colt. And she hoped desperately that the two of them would be proved right. That Midnight would perform well at the rodeo, that he wouldn't be hurt, and that he'd come home and be a little easier to manage.

But she wished it had been Colt who'd told her the story, not Gracie. Funny how, now that she was living in his trailer, she felt more distant from Colt than ever.

Maybe he regretted inviting her and the kids to the Belt rodeo. And she should really take the kids to visit her mother. She didn't want the disagreement between them to turn into a full-fledged rift.

A text early Sunday morning helped Leah make up her mind. Made the finals! Steer wrestling and bull riding both! Can't wait to see you...

With bubbles of happiness and excitement replacing her earlier fears, Leah woke the children and helped them dress in their jeans and Western shirts. She didn't have boots for them yet, so they had to wear sneakers. She made up for it by promising to buy them cowboy hats later.

They had breakfast in the trailer and were on the road by eight-thirty. Leah wanted to arrive in time for the parade at eleven. She'd taken the kids to the Calgary Stampede two years ago, but they'd been so young, they didn't really remember anything.

The Stampede was a big, splashy, ten-day event in Calgary, nothing like the small-town rodeo at Belt. But Leah thought they would enjoy the small-town event just as much, if not more.

During the drive she and the kids sang songs and played "I Spy" until Davey fell asleep. Then Leah started a CD of Robert Munsch stories for Jill, while her daughter followed along with the books.

Two and a half hours later they arrived in Belt, just in time to find a parking spot, get out their lawn chairs and find a spot along the main street to watch the parade.

The parade was open, which meant anyone could participate. There were baton twirlers and a bagpipe band, men driving tractors and muscle cars, and people dressed in costumes tossing candy to the children.

Davey and Jill loved that part the most, next to the parade of horses. For Leah, the best part was watching the simple joy on her children's faces.

When the parade ended, they joined the crowds and walked over to the park where Jill and Davey participated in the kiddie rodeo, an informal event where the kids tried to lasso fake cows for the chance to win a prize. Once they'd each had a turn, Leah bought them hot dogs and staked a spot on the bleachers to watch the rodeo.

She was so glad she'd come. She'd missed all of this. Small-town rodeos really were the best. You could see the excitement from right up close. Behind them was a pen of bucking horses. She could swear the horses had as much pent-up excitement as the cowboys who were waiting to ride them. Most of the bucking stock had been supplied by a rodeo contracting outfit from Sidney, Montana. She tried to pick out Midnight, and finally saw the stallion being loaded into the chutes, Ace and Colt keeping a close eye on him.

"It smells like Thunder Ranch, Mommy."

She squeezed Jill's hand. "I know. Isn't it wonderful?"

The first event was bareback riding, and watching the cowboys milling around the chutes, Leah felt her own stomach squeeze with nerves and anticipation. They had so much invested on just eight seconds of performance.

Leah had wondered if Davey would be too young, if his attention would wander, but between the antics of the rodeo clown, the joking of the announcer and the actual rides on the bucking horses, he was enthralled.

For the first two rides, both cowboys managed to hold on for eight seconds and earn respectable scores. Then it was Midnight's turn. Just Colt and Ace were handling him, and he seemed high-spirited, but not out of control. Even from a distance of about fifty yards,

Leah could swear she saw a wicked gleam in his eyes. She sure wouldn't want to be the cowboy who'd drawn him.

The announcer introduced him with relish. "And, folks, I'm happy to say that after an absence of several years, The Midnight Express is back with us today, compliments of his new owners at Thunder Ranch. Most cowboys here remember this horse—his lineage goes back to the great hall-of-fame bucking horse Five Minutes to Midnight. Good luck to the cowboy who gets to ride him today, Mr. Ethan Radler from Newkirk, Oklahoma. Ethan's got his own claim to fame—"

"Mommy, you're hurting my hand." Jill wriggled her fingers free and gave her mother an affronted frown.

"Sorry, peanut, I'm just excited. You see that cowboy climbing the fence over there by Colt and Ace? He's going to try to ride Midnight for eight seconds."

"But Midnight won't let him. He'll buck him off." Jill sounded so confident, Leah had to smile.

"Are you sure?"

"He bucked off Colt, and he's the best cowboy in the world. So there."

So there, indeed. Leah wondered what Colt would think of the fact that her daughter held him in such high esteem. Would Jill's faith make Colt want to live up to her image of him as a role model? Or would it just scare him off?

A few weeks ago, she would have bet money on the latter. But Colt was changing, and she was excited by the direction he seemed to be heading in. Possibilities were opening up for him—and for them—that made her positively giddy to think about.

Or was she just suffering from rodeo fever? She had

to admit, the tension was escalating with each second it took for Ethan to get himself into position for the ride.

Midnight's energy was palpable as he tossed his head and snorted, resisting the touch of even Ace and Colt as they tried to get him to settle enough for Ethan to mount.

But finally they were ready, and Ethan gave the nod for the chute to be opened. Quickly, the wranglers jumped to the side as Midnight blasted free. His speed seemed to catch Ethan by surprise and as the cowboy struggled for balance, Midnight suddenly threw up his front legs, then rocked back.

Ethan was completely out of position and when Midnight added a twist to his repertoire, the unfortunate cowboy went flying sideways.

No eight-second whistle.

He'd been the victor, and Midnight sure seemed to know it. He strutted his stuff for several seconds before allowing the pick-up men to corral him out of the arena.

While the crowd clapped for the disappointed Ethan, privately Leah clapped for Midnight. He'd been magnificent! Even Ace must have been thrilled by his performance.

There were five more rides after Midnight's, and while Leah enjoyed them all, she couldn't focus with the same intensity as earlier. She'd been hoping that after Midnight's performance, Colt would come and find them in the stands. But he was probably busy preparing for his steer-wrestling event.

And then the last bareback rider was done and it was time for steer wrestling. Leah was on the edge of her seat when Colt was finally introduced, second to last.

"And now, ladies and gentlemen, we have a local cowboy who needs no introduction—but I'll give him one anyway. Colt Hart, from Thunder Ranch is an eight-time NFR qualifier. He will be the man to beat, especially with Ace Hart teaming up with him today."

"That's Colt's brother," Jill said. "Right, Mom?"

"Yes. His job is to keep the steer running in a straight path." Her mouth went dry as a wad of cotton candy as she spotted Colt, waiting behind the barrier, dressed in his trademark red shirt and black hat.

Jill pulled on her hand. "What's a steer?"

"It's a boy cow that isn't big enough to be a bull." She wasn't going to attempt to explain castration to them right now. If they kept spending time at Thunder Ranch, they'd learn soon enough.

"Is that the steer?" Jill pointed to the chute.

"Yes. He'll get a head start, and then Colt has to chase after him and wrestle him to the ground."

Now Davey was tugging on her hand. "He has big howns on his head. Will they huwt?"

"Don't worry about Colt. He knows what he's doing." Leah said a little prayer for him, just the same. Her gaze was fixed on Colt, waiting for the signal...

And suddenly the steer was running into the arena, with Colt in hot pursuit. One second he was on his horse, the next sliding down, hooking his arm around one horn, then reaching for the second.

Another blink of the eyes and the steer was on the ground with all four hooves pointed in the same direction.

"Three-point-five seconds!" The crowd erupted in cheers at this, the fastest time of the day.

Leah and the kids stood up and clapped and cheered. Colt spotted them and waved his hat in their direction, before leaving the arena.

All Leah wanted to do was run after him and tell

him how proud she was, but the next event was saddle bronc riding and she waited for it to finish before suggesting to the kids that they take a break.

"Don't want to go home." Davey, who never pouted, was sticking out his bottom lip in a fair imitation of one.

"We aren't going home. There's still barrel races and bull riding to come. The best part. We'll just go to the washroom and get some more snacks." And maybe find Colt…?

Leah took the kids to the washroom first, then headed for the concession stand. As she walked, she scanned the crowd for Colt's distinctive red shirt. No luck.

She bought the kids orange drinks and popcorn, then wandered beyond the arena toward the stock pens. A line of trucks and stock trailers were parked on the other side of a gravel road. She stopped when she heard some voices coming from behind the Thunder Ranch rig. That sure sounded like Colt.

As she was about to step forward to investigate, Ace suddenly emerged from a group of wranglers hanging out at the stock pens.

"Leah." He called her name sharply.

"Hi, Ace. Sorry, didn't see you there. What about Midnight, huh? He's some horse. You must be so proud."

"More like relieved that he didn't get hurt." Ace smiled at the kids, then shot a worried glance toward the trailer that Leah had been heading for.

"How about I buy you guys a drink?" Like a good cutting horse, he came up from behind and began herding them back toward the concessions.

"Actually, I thought I heard Colt over there." She gestured toward the trailer. "We were going to wish him l—"

Her words trailed as Colt suddenly came into view. He was talking to a blond woman who looked like a slightly older version of Taylor Swift. They'd been on the other side of the Thunder Ranch rig and were now walking slowly toward the guest parking lot. The woman was dressed in expensive Western duds, and she was acting as if nothing else existed for her in that moment but Colt. His attention was just as riveted on her.

Suddenly they stopped. They were totally into one another now. If a thunderstorm started, Leah didn't think they'd notice. And then the woman was throwing her arms around Colt, and Colt was pulling her in close—

Leah couldn't watch anymore. Jill and Davey had noticed nothing, but Ace had. She could see sympathy, laced with anger, in his eyes.

"Um...I don't suppose that woman is a family member I haven't met?"

"Never seen her before. I'm sorry, Leah. I really thought Colt was changing his ways. And that you were the reason."

Yeah. He wasn't the only one who had thought that.

Ace put a brotherly arm around her shoulders. "Let me get you that drink."

"Actually, I think it's time the kids and I headed home." She felt numb, but she knew from experience that the shock would wear off, followed by the terrible pain of betrayal. Oh, she'd walked this walk before, she knew exactly how it went.

Colt hadn't planned how his meeting with Janet would go. All they'd agreed to over the phone was that they would meet up during the rodeo finals on Sunday.

"I'm not sure if I'll bring Evan with me or not. I need to discuss this with Justin."

Justin Greenway was her husband. And Colt had understood, even though it rankled, that this other man got to decide where and when he could meet his own son.

But then, given his lack of involvement over the past twelve years, he hadn't earned the right to make any decisions where Evan was concerned.

And now Janet was questioning his change of heart.

"Why now, Colt? That's what I need to understand. If this is just a whim, I can't risk Evan getting hurt."

She was still a beauty, Janet, but he felt none of his old attraction. She was the mother of his son and she'd raised Evan, and for that he could only be grateful.

"I've fallen in love with someone. She's a wonderful woman with two children of her own. But when I'm with her I can't help but ask myself, what do I have to offer her and her kids?"

Janet put her hands on her hips. She wasn't convinced, but she was listening at least. "Go on."

Colt started feeling desperate. If he didn't persuade Janet that his intentions were honorable, then everything would be lost. He had to be honest and open with her. No matter how hard it was. "Looking back, I think I kind of gave up on myself after I found out about our baby. You didn't need me to raise our son, so I figured I wasn't worth much."

"That's pretty stupid logic. If you'd asked, I would have given you visitation rights."

"Sounds so simple when you put it that way. But that letter your lawyer sent me—well, it seemed like money was the only help you needed or wanted."

"At the time, that's probably exactly how I felt. It was only later, when Evan grew older and started asking questions, that I realized he might need more from his birth father. One thing I never did was lie to him. And Justin agreed with me on that."

"Did—did Evan ever ask to meet me?"

She hesitated. Then nodded. "I kept putting him off. I didn't want you to hurt him."

There was something left unsaid in that sentence. Colt thought back to the weekend he'd spent with Janet all those years ago. When they'd parted, he knew he hadn't promised her anything. He never did.

But maybe she had thought he would call sometime. Maybe he had hurt her back then, before she met Justin, and maybe she'd been afraid he would do the exact same with Evan.

"It's taken me a lot of time, but I've finally grown up. If you and Justin allow me to meet Evan, I promise you that I will be as big or as little a piece of that boy's life as he wants me to be. I'll put his interests first, and I may let him down a time or two, but if I do I'll apologize and try to do better. I've never been a father, and I'm late to the game, but I'd like to try, Janet, if you'll please give me a chance."

Tears welled in her eyes. But she didn't say anything, just started walking away. He followed, using the opportunity to continue to plead his case.

"I don't blame you for being angry with me. I didn't treat you well, and I've waited a long time to step forward. Is there anything I can say or do to convince you—"

"Colt." She quieted him with a hand to his arm. "You don't need to say another word. I've already decided to introduce you to Evan, and what better time than now? He's sitting in the stands with his father."

"You really mean that?" He actually felt his body start to tremble.

"I do." She gave him a rueful smile. "I suppose you're nervous. Don't be. Evan is a really neat kid. You're going to get along just fine."

And then she put her arms around him and gave him a big hug. Colt gratefully wrapped his arms around her. And just at that moment, from the corner of his eye, he noticed Leah and her kids walking with Ace.

He pulled away from Janet's embrace and considered waving them over to tell them the good news. But they didn't seem to have noticed him, which was just as well. They were walking in the opposite direction now, probably heading back to their seats for the second half of the show.

He was supposed to be getting ready to compete himself, but he couldn't care less about his standings at this moment. He waited as Janet sent a text message to her husband, asking him to bring Evan to the Thunder Ranch transport truck.

"Evan came to this rodeo to see you," Janet said. "He's followed your career, but never seen you perform in person. We told him there was a chance that he'd meet you today. He's very excited."

"He doesn't hate me?"

"Not yet. But I have to warn you, anger may kick in at some point. Then again, he's a pretty easygoing kid. And he's had a nice life. Justin has been a good father."

"I'm glad to hear that," Colt said. And he was. At the same time he felt a searing jealousy for all that he'd missed. Even though it was his own damn fault, it still hurt.

Janet stiffened, then started waving her arm. "There they are."

Colt spotted them at that moment, too. A red-headed man with slender shoulders walking alongside a sandy-haired boy, who looked nervous as hell.

I am too, kid, he thought to himself. *I am, too.*

Chapter Sixteen

What do you say to a twelve-year-old son you'd never met before? If this was awkward for Colt, a thirty-two-year-old man, he could only imagine how much worse it must be for Evan. The kid, about five-five already, had his fingers stuffed in the front pockets of his jeans. He kept looking from Colt, to his sneakers, then back at Colt.

"Hey, Evan." Colt stuck out his hand. "It's good to finally meet you."

He'd pictured his son hundreds of times in his head, but seeing him now, in person, Colt felt a weird, warm feeling flood over him. He'd always wondered if he'd be able to pick the kid out in a crowd. The answer was yes.

Evan looked at his mother first, then Justin, before releasing his fingers from the pocket of his jeans and shaking Colt's hand.

"This is weird, huh? I have to say…I have pictures of me on the ranch when I was your age and, well—" Colt shook his head "—let's just say there's a pretty strong resemblance."

Justin stepped forward then. "Hi, I'm Janet's husband."

No name. Just *Janet's husband*. Staking his claim, Colt supposed. He gave the guy a friendly smile, hoping to set him at ease. He had no interest in moving in on this man's territory. Not where his wife was concerned, anyway.

"Nice to meet you, too, Justin." The guy had a firm grip, and his light blue eyes telegraphed a warning along with the hand shake. *Don't hurt my family.*

Colt understood the man's protectiveness, even as he resented it.

Janet joined her family, moving in between Justin and Evan, then placing a hand on her son's shoulder. They were almost the same height, but it wouldn't be long before Evan outgrew her. He was only twelve, and Colt's height hadn't leveled off until he was almost eighteen.

"So…how are you liking the rodeo so far?"

"It's okay."

He caught a glimpse of his son's eyes that time, and been a little shocked to see the same gold-green eyes that stared back at him every day when he shaved.

"Do you ride, Evan?"

Before the boy could answer, Justin said, "Evan's into baseball. He started with T-ball when he was four. Now he plays shortstop and he's got the best average and the best slugging percentage on his team."

Evan's ears turned red and Janet gave her husband's arm a little tug. "Maybe we should give these two a few minutes to get acquainted. What do you think, Evan? Do you want a minute alone with…Colt?"

Evan shrugged. "I guess."

Colt felt his mouth go dry. He had no experience with kids of any ages—Jill and Davey excepted. He didn't think the tactics that worked with a five-year-old and a two-year-old would go far with a boy on the verge of adolescence. He took a deep breath. *Just talk. Let him get to know you.*

"How'd you like to meet the number one horse at Thunder Ranch?"

"The Midnight Express?"

Finally, a spark of interest on the boy's face. Maybe he was more interested in rodeo than his father thought.

"Yup. He used to be a real rodeo legend and we're hoping he'll be one again."

"Yeah, it'd be cool to see him. Can I touch him?"

"That's up to Midnight to decide. But I have something in my truck that might help." He started walking and Evan stepped in beside him.

"So we'll see you back here in about fifteen minutes?" Janet called after them.

Colt paused to give her a reassuring nod. When he reached his vehicle, he grabbed a couple of horse treats from his glove compartment.

"Nice truck," Evan said.

"Yeah, isn't it? I won it at a rodeo in Oklahoma last month."

"So…you're a full-time cowboy, right?" His gaze went to the buckle on Colt's belt.

"That's right. I've got a drawer full of buckles like this one. I've been doing this a long time—since I was eighteen." Colt started heading toward Midnight's pen. Ace had taken care to have the stallion separated from the other bucking horses, most of which were mares. He could see the horse tracking his approach from fifty yards away.

"So, you like, live on the road, traveling from one rodeo to another?"

"I spend a lot of time like that. But I also have a home. Thunder Ranch, near Roundup. We run a few

hundred cattle and also have a bucking stock operation—horses and bulls. Since my father died about ten
years ago, Mom runs the place." Colt swallowed. "When
the time comes, I know she'd love to meet you."

"She'd be my grandmother, huh? That's bizarre."

"Yeah. I guess it wouldn't feel so strange if I had
asked to be a part of your life right from the start. I
wish I had."

Evan was silent for a bit, then he surprised Colt by
saying, "Thanks for sending those checks, anyway.
Mom puts some of the money away for college. The rest
we use for stuff like my baseball and clothes for school.
And I guess next year—" he grimaced "—braces."

"You don't need to thank me for that money, Evan.
Though I really appreciate that you did. It's just what
fathers do. And I wish I'd done a lot more."

They stopped. They'd reached the fence. Midnight's
ears twitched, as he trained his wary eyes on them. Colt
pulled the horse cookie out of his pocket and handed
it to Evan.

"Ever fed a horse before?"

"No."

"Keep your hand open, like this." Colt demonstrated.

"He isn't coming."

"Give him a minute. You're an unfamiliar face, with
an unfamiliar scent. Midnight suffered at the hand of
a cruel foreman for a few years and he's learned to be
cautious about the human race."

As he said those words, Colt looked at his son. He
hoped Evan hadn't learned the same lesson, thanks to
an absent father.

"I was twenty when I met your mother. I should have
been old enough to do the right thing back then. But

I guess I still had a lot of growing up to do. I figured you had a mother and a father, so I wasn't needed. And maybe I wasn't, in the strictest sense. But you were still my son, and I should have fought to be a part of your life."

It was a long speech for Colt. His second of the day. He could feel tears gathering in his eyes this time, though. And he glanced down at the ground and blinked them away.

Evan didn't say anything. He'd turned his face away, too. Maybe for the same reason?

And then Midnight started walking toward them. Just watching him move, Colt was struck again by the beauty of this animal. He was a special horse, Midnight.

He came right up to them, snorting at the scent of the treat.

"Hey, boy," Colt crooned, "don't be afraid. There's someone here I'd like you to meet."

Midnight hesitated. Snorted again. Looked like he was going to leave, then changed his mind and approached the boy's outstretched hand.

"He's eating it!"

"Stay nice and calm. Don't spook him."

"Good boy, Midnight," Evan said. He turned to Colt, a genuine smile on his face, the first Colt had seen on his son's face.

A tidal wave of warmth flooded over him then, just like it had when he'd first met Evan. Only now Colt understood what it was, and what it meant.

It was love.

COLT MADE SURE THAT they were back to meet Evan's parents in the allotted fifteen minutes. The four of them chatted for a few minutes, and then when it was time for them to leave, Colt gathered his courage and asked if he could maybe watch one of Evan's baseball games sometime. When Evan smiled, he knew he'd done the right thing and Janet promised to send him the schedule by email.

Watching them leave, Colt had the hardest time not giving in to a flood of tears. The last time he'd cried had been when his father had died. That was a period of his life he didn't like looking back on. But it was hard not to wish that his father had been able to meet Evan before he passed.

If Colt had done the right thing from the beginning, he would have.

"Colt! What the hell are you doing?" Ace was running toward him, from the direction of the stands. "Barrel racing is just ending and your next event is about to start."

Colt rubbed his jaw and took a deep breath. He felt as if hours had passed since he'd met Janet at his truck, but really it had only been about thirty minutes. "Have you seen Leah and the kids?"

Ace looked at him as if he was an idiot. "They left."

"What do you mean they left? I just saw them a little while ago."

"Yeah, they were here. But when she saw you with that blonde she decided she needed to go home." The look on his brother's face was now pure disdain. "How can you be so stupid?"

At first Colt was confused. But then he realized by "that blonde" Ace meant "Janet." So Leah had seen them talking and had assumed he was putting the moves on her?

Why would she do that?

Then again, why wouldn't she? He had a reputation as a ladies' man at the rodeo and he had no one to blame for that but himself.

He'd considered telling Leah that he was hoping to meet his son at this rodeo. But he'd been afraid to jinx it by talking about it. Now he saw how foolish he'd been.

"We've got to go home," he told his brother anxiously. "I've got to talk to her."

"But you're not done here."

"Leah's more important...."

Ace grabbed his arm. "Should have thought about that before you started chatting up the blonde. Right now, you have a job to do."

"So what? I couldn't care less about my standings right now."

"Don't tell me you're going to start screwing up on the rodeo circuit, too. This is the one thing you've always done right."

Colt glared at him. There wasn't time, and this wasn't the place, to explain everything to his brother. But it would be downright stupid of him to try to ride a bull when his head was someplace else. The meeting with Evan had been emotional enough. Now, knowing Leah was upset with him, there was no way he'd be able to concentrate on anything until he'd cleared up their misunderstanding.

He yanked his arm free. "Ace, when are you going to stop trying to run my life?"

He thought his brother would finally back down. Instead, Ace got right in his face, fists clenched. "Maybe when you start doing a proper job on your own."

Hell, Ace was prepared to fight him on this.

Colt glared at his brother. And then something occurred to him. Ace was right. Colt *had* made a mess of his life up to this point. Maybe follow-through began here. Doing a job even though his heart wasn't in it, just because he'd made the commitment.

The fight went out of him. He heaved a big sigh.

"You win, Ace. I'll do it."

THE TROUBLE BEGAN on his dismount. Colt managed to ride Western Twister for the entire eight seconds, during which time the bull lived up to his name. After a series of front-end drops and back-end kicks, he started twisting to the right so fast Colt figured the bull was trying to rocket him up to the stratosphere.

The whistle sounded. He was done, thank God. Now he could get in his truck and drive home to Leah.

Oh, yeah. One problem. He was still on the bull. And getting off was often the most dangerous part of the job. At least the bull had stopped twisting.

Ahead of him, the rodeo clown approached with a barrel to distract the bull, while two pickup men came from the side to help scoop Colt up to safety.

Colt reached for the saddle of the nearest pickup man, then swore as he misjudged the distance and started to fall. Even before he hit the ground, the bull was on him, bearing down with his head, oblivious to the clown and the pickup men trying bravely to distract him.

Colt attempted rolling to safety, but one of the bull's horns caught on his safety vest. With a toss of the bull's head, Colt was flying again, this time with no bull underneath him.

God help me, but this is going to hurt.

And then all went black.

COLT HAD NEVER SEEN Ace's face so pale. "Are you okay, bro?"

A weak smile replaced the frown. "I'm not the one in the hospital."

Colt tried to look around, but his neck muscles protested. He saw enough, though. "Thought I recognized the decor."

"Yeah, the ambulance took you to Great Falls. They were worried about internal injuries, but you seem to be fine. I guess those ribs did their job, though I hate to tell you that one of them is cracked."

Colt put a hand to the bandages swaddling his chest. "So that's why it hurts to breathe." He thought back to the accident. He remembered the ride and the whistle, but not much after that. "So what was my score?"

"Trust you to ask that. It was seventy-nine."

"Not too good."

"It was good enough."

"You mean I won the event?"

"And All-Around Cowboy, too."

"Well, hell, that's good news." He tried to prop himself up on his elbows, then winced with pain. "Any chance you could give me a hand?"

"None at all."

"What do you mean?"

"I mean you're not going anywhere. You're booked in for the night. Mani, pedi, the whole nine yards."

"No. I need to see Leah. And what about Midnight?"

"The vet working the rodeo is a friend of mine. He's keeping an eye on Midnight until we're ready to drive home."

"I'm ready now."

"You are not. You were unconscious for bit, and the doc wants to make sure you didn't suffer a concussion."

Ace sighed. "Look, I'm sorry I insisted you ride that bull. It was your call to make, not mine. And I feel—"

"Oh, shut up, would you? You're too smart to think this accident is your fault. I ride bulls for living. Statistically speaking, I'm going to end up in the hospital every now and then. But if you're not letting me go home tonight, at least get me my phone so I can call Leah."

Chapter Seventeen

Packing their belongings and leaving Colt's trailer didn't take long. It would have gone faster, though, if her kids weren't so upset. Davey had cried for half an hour in the car because they left the rodeo early.

Then he'd fallen asleep, thank goodness. And now it was Jill giving her a hard time.

"But I like Thunder Ranch. I don't want to go."

"You knew from the start that this was temporary, peanut." Leah grabbed the toothbrushes out of the bathroom and added them to the open suitcase on the kitchen counter. "Colt needs his trailer, so we have to leave."

"But we're *always* leaving."

Leah froze. Put a hand to her chest, as if she could find the source of the pain that was stabbing at her heart. "Well, this time we're not leaving. We're going back."

"Going back where?"

"To Grandma's house. Now get in the car, Jill. I'll load these suitcases in the trunk and we'll see if we can't get to Grandma's in time for dinner."

Leah thought about phoning ahead to warn her mother they were coming. She didn't question whether her mother would take them in. Leah knew she would. Oh, there'd be a price to pay at some point, but she would endure the lectures. And she would do her best to make sure they happened out of the children's hearing range. The reason she didn't phone was because she had no idea what to say. Maybe, in person, it would be easier.

Of course, it wasn't.

Standing on her mother's front porch twenty minutes later, with the kids and suitcases beside her, she could feel her eyes fill with tears. She tried to speak, but her voice had abandoned her.

Her mother stood at the open door. The aroma of roasting chicken was in the background, as well as the soundtrack of a popular musical: *Mamma Mia! Here we go again.*

The kids ran inside. They'd watched the DVD many times with Leah, and even though they didn't understand the story, they loved to dance to the music.

Leah tried again to talk.

"Come in, sweetheart," her mother said. "I think you need a glass of wine and a nice family dinner. How does that sound?"

Leah started to cry.

HALF AN HOUR LATER, Leah had that glass of wine in her hands and was relaxing on the sofa while the kids danced to the last scene of the musical, when she heard her iPhone chime.

Her mother, who had refused to allow her to help with the dinner, was in the kitchen.

Leah tried to resist. But the temptation was too much. She picked up her phone and saw a text message from Colt.

Something came up at the rodeo. I won't be home until later tomorrow morning. See you then!

She deleted the message, then turned off her phone. Something had come up all right. Something with blond hair and a nice curvy body... What was he thinking? That she wouldn't figure it out? Did every man in this world think it was their right to sleep with any woman stupid enough to have them?

The credits began to roll then, and her mom called them to the dinner table. Leah switched off the television, then helped the kids wash their hands.

At the table, they found a platter of roasted chicken, mashed potatoes and gravy, corn and peas.

"How do you do it, Mom? An hour after we show up on your doorstep and you have a beautiful meal all ready for us. Doesn't this look delicious, Jill?"

"I love corn," Jill answered.

And Davey loved peas. He liked to mash them with his fork and eat them one by one. Leah knew it was no coincidence that her mother had prepared her children's favorite vegetables. She gazed fondly at her mom, who was busy cutting Jill's chicken and didn't notice.

"There's apple crisp for dessert, too, so make sure you leave a little room."

And that was *Leah's* favorite. Her mom truly had covered all the bases.

During the meal, the kids were full of talk about the rodeo. Leah did her best to put the random comments into context for her mother. They told their grandmother about the parade, about the kiddie rodeo, then about the cowboys and the rodeo clown.

"And Colt was there. He rustled a steer," Jill said proudly.

"Wrestled," Leah corrected.

"And Midnight bucked!" Davey announced, lifting his fork in a victory pump.

"Sounds like quite the day." There was a question in her mother's eyes as she looked at Leah. She had to be wondering why they had ended up on her doorstep after such a fun outing.

It wasn't until later, when the kids had been bathed and put into their old bedrooms, that Leah finally had a chance to have a proper conversation with her mom.

"I owe you an apology." She curled up next to her mother on the sofa. "You had every right to be upset about the divorce. I just feel like such a failure when you tell me I didn't try hard enough. Because I *did* try, Mom. I really did."

"I believe you. And I didn't mean to make you feel like a failure. You're anything but. Even as a child, whenever you fell down, or hit an obstacle, you always pushed yourself back to your feet and tried again. It did hurt, though, when you picked Thunder Ranch rather than my home after your house flooded."

"I'm sorry. That was a mistake." A *huge* mistake. She'd tell her mom about what happened with Colt someday—when it no longer hurt so much.

"Well, the past few days gave me time to think and I realize I may have pushed too hard with my advice. But I believed it was my duty, Leah."

"Your duty?"

"As your mother. You see, when I was newly married to your father, there was a period of about five years when I was very unhappy. I thought about leaving. Might have done so, too, if it wasn't for the counsel of your grandmother."

Leah had never thought her parents' marriage was perfect. But she'd never guessed that it had come to the brink of dissolution, either. "What happened, Mom?"

"Nothing like what Jackson put you through. Your

father was always faithful and loyal. But I had been raised in Great Falls and I had a terrible time adjusting to life on a ranch. I was so lonely and, though I didn't want to admit it to your father, the cattle and horses scared me."

"Poor Mom." She'd always guessed that her mother hadn't been so fond of ranch life, but never that she'd been *this* unhappy.

"Then you were born, a beautiful, happy baby. I should have been happy, too, but I couldn't sleep and I was crying all the time."

Leah hadn't felt that way after her babies were born, but she'd read magazine articles describing those symptoms. "You had postpartum depression."

"Yes. But it wasn't diagnosed at the time. I just thought I was unhappy because I'd married the wrong man. I came so close to leaving, but your grandma came to visit. She stayed for several months and helped me with the chores and the night feedings. During the day she talked to me about the sort of commitment that's needed to make a marriage last—and to make a family strong."

"And so you stayed. And you were a wonderful wife and mother."

"Thank you for saying that." Her mom patted her cheek. "It means more than you know."

"It's true. I'm only realizing now how much I took you for granted." Her mother had always been busy, but at the same time, when Leah needed her, she was there. Leah had grown up thinking homemade cinnamon buns and hot chocolate after school were nothing special. And she couldn't count the number of times her mother had patiently helped with her school assignments.

"But Mom…did you ever think you'd sacrificed too much for us?"

"I lived to be very grateful that I'd stayed."

"But if you hated the ranch…"

"Over the years I grew to love many things about it. No, Leah, I have absolutely zero regrets about staying with your father. But it's because I went through that rough patch that I felt I needed to give you the same sort of support that I'd received from your grandmother."

It made so much sense to Leah, now. She wished her mother had told her this earlier. "I wonder how a woman is supposed to know a rough patch from an irreconcilable difference?"

"That's a good question. I suspect it has something to do with respect and trust. When those are lost, I don't think any marriage can survive."

Her mother was so wise. Because that was exactly what had happened today at the rodeo. Leah had lost her trust in Colt. And she hadn't even realized, until it happened, how much she loved him.

IT WASN'T UNTIL 9:00 a.m. on Monday morning that Colt finally got the green light to go home. Ace had Midnight loaded in the trailer, and was waiting in the truck as Colt strode out of the hospital into the bright sunshine of a beautiful June day. Colt wasn't feeling very bright or sunshiny himself. Not just his ribs, but his whole body ached after his tussle with the bull.

Plus he was beyond worried about Leah. She hadn't replied to his text message last night, nor had she answered any of his calls.

He was glad to see a cup of coffee waiting for him in the cup holder when he climbed into the passenger side of the truck.

"You want me to drive?"

Ace shook his head and grinned. "You're kidding, right? Just sit back and rest. You shouldn't even be out of bed yet."

Colt ignored him and pulled out his phone. No messages. He kept it in his hand, just in case.

"Why the big sigh?" Ace checked in his mirror, before merging onto the road toward home.

"Leah isn't answering her phone. It would be nice to know she got home safely."

"Well you can stop worrying. She did."

"How do you know?"

"Mom. I phoned her after I called Flynn last night to give her an update."

Colt realized he should have called his mother, too. But he'd had a lot on his mind. His son, for one. Their first meeting had gone better than he'd hoped. Better than he deserved. Janet was right. Evan was a real nice kid. She—and Justin—had done a great job raising him.

He was dying to tell Leah all about it. Why wasn't she answering her phone? Unable to resist, he checked for messages again.

"Might as well save your time," Ace said drily.

"Why?" Colt studied his brother's face carefully. He was wearing that know-it-all expression that so often drove Colt crazy.

"She saw you with the blonde, right? She's probably pissed as hell, and who could blame her? Damn it, Colt, I thought you were—" Ace slammed a hand against the steering wheel. "Aw, forget it. You never listen to me, anyway."

"Well, you don't know everything."

"I know you were hugging a beautiful blonde after inviting Leah and her kids to watch you at the rodeo."

"But…it wasn't like that. Janet is someone I knew a long time ago."

"I meet old friends all the time. I don't hug them the way you were hugging that Janet woman."

Colt's temper flared. "Maybe you would if they'd had your baby."

"What!" Ace gripped the wheel tightly, then shot a fireball at Colt with his eyes. "When did this happen?"

"Twelve years ago." Colt had planned on his mother being the first member of the family he told. Damn him and his hot temper. Now Ace would tear a strip off his hide and while Colt knew he deserved his brother's approbation, he was sick and tired of Ace acting like his father.

But the expected words of condemnation didn't come. Ace was quiet for a full five minutes before he spoke again. And when he did, his voice was full of concern.

"How did it happen?"

"I met Janet at the Belt rodeo, thirteen years ago. We met up on the Friday night, at a bar in town, and ended up spending most of the weekend together. We didn't see one another after that. The next time I heard from her was nine months later when I received a registered letter from her lawyer."

Ace whistled. "She didn't call you personally?"

"Nah. She'd met someone shortly after our affair. They'd fallen in love and were getting married. The fellow's name is Justin Greenway. A decent enough guy. He agreed to raise Janet's baby as his son, so according to the letter I got from the lawyer, all that was required from me were monthly child support payments."

"And you've been paying those?"

Colt nodded. "Since I was twenty years old."

His brother shot another look at him—this one seemed to hold respect. "Who else knows about this?"

"No one. I considered telling Dad. But you'd just been accepted at vet school and he was so proud of you. I figured he'd just see me as even more of a loser than he already did."

"Dad never saw you that way. How could he? You're an amazingly talented guy."

"You mean talented at attracting trouble." And those were his father's exact words. They were branded in Colt's memory from repeated usage.

"I can't believe you went through all this on your own."

"Leah was the first person I told."

"She means a lot to you," Ace said, like he was only now figuring this out.

"I love her. Until I met her, I never saw the need to rise above the opinion that everyone else seemed to have of me."

"And that's why you were talking with Janet at the rodeo?"

"I needed her okay, so I could finally meet my son. Which I did. And he's fantastic." Colt felt a warm glow inside, just recalling the special moments they'd spent together. "I'm going to watch him play baseball next week."

"That's terrific." Ace shook his head. "You know what this means? Mom is already a grandmother. And I'm an uncle… Holy crap. This is terrific news, Colt."

Yeah, it was. But now that he knew what Leah had seen, and what she'd surmised, Colt was more desperate than ever to talk to her.

WHEN ACE AND COLT pulled into Thunder Ranch, Gracie was waiting for them. She started talking as soon as they stepped out of the truck, telling them that the clients who had booked Midnight's stud services that week had already arrived and unloaded their four mares into the pasture.

"Ed Fowley wanted to talk to you before the breeding commences." Gracie was addressing Ace, but her eyes were on the bandages wrapped around Colt's chest. "What happened to *you?*"

"The usual. I got kicked around by a bull."

"Glad to see you're still standing." She turned back to Ace. "I told Ed to go to Roundup, grab a coffee and a muffin and come back at noon."

Ace checked his watch. "Good, we've got an hour then. Let's unload Midnight and get him comfortable. I'm planning to try a supervised breeding today, Gracie. Since he kicked ass at the rodeo on Sunday, Midnight's been acting like another horse. He loaded like a dream this morning."

"You sure you brought home the right horse?"

"I told you Midnight missed the rodeo," Colt felt compelled to point out.

"True enough. But he still could have been injured," Ace replied.

Colt supposed this was one subject where the two of them would never agree. But their relationship had shifted during their two-hour drive. Ace was no longer just his superior older brother, but someone he might count on as a friend.

When Gracie started preparing to unload Midnight, Colt moved to help her. Ace stopped him with a hand on his shoulder.

"We'll handle this. I know you have someone you need to talk to."

Relieved, Colt thanked his brother, then headed for the trailer. It hurt to run, but he couldn't stop himself. He was desperate to see her. But when he arrived at his Airstream, all was quiet. He knocked, then opened the door.

The place was pristine. Every one of Leah's and the kids' belongings were gone.

"They've moved back to Leah's mother's house."

His own mother must have followed him here, because she was now sitting at the picnic table. He closed the door to the trailer.

"Hi, Mom." He sank down heavily onto the bench across the table from her.

"Are you okay, son?"

"I'll heal." The day was catching up to him. His body was screaming at him to lie down. But he needed to find Leah. "Is that where she is now? At her mother's?"

"Tell me something first, Colt. Do you love her?"

"I do. And I have more news for you, Mom. I had an ulterior motive for going to the rodeo in Belt last weekend. I wanted to meet someone special—my son."

His mother stared back at him, speechless. He reached for her hand and squeezed it tightly.

"We'll talk about this later, okay? But I really need to see Leah, because she saw something and interpreted it the wrong way."

Sarah blinked. "You are going to be the death of me one day, son."

"I hope not, Mom. Because I love you a lot. And I'm looking forward to the day when I can introduce you to your grandson. He's twelve and he loves baseball."

Sarah's eyes rounded in shock. "Twelve?"

"I'll explain later," he promised. "Leah?"

Sarah let out a long sigh. "She's in the office, finishing up her work for me. She's a terrific gal. You better set things right with her, Colt."

He was already off the bench, starting to run. "I'll try."

LEAH REVIEWED THE printouts one more time, checking for errors. There were none. She'd finished computerizing the Thunder Ranch accounts and had printed out the latest monthly reports for Sarah to send to the bank.

From now on she'd be able to keep up with the accounting for the ranch by spending a half day per week, with a little extra at reporting dates and income tax time. She needed more clients, but she had several meetings lined up and she was confident that more work would follow.

After dropping the kids off at their babysitter's that morning, she'd also taken time to call her landlord. The insurance company was scheduled to examine the damage this week. After that, the landlord would organize repairs. Hopefully she and the kids would be able to move in within the next month, or so.

Meanwhile, her mother had assured her they were welcome to stay with her.

Leah knew she ought to be feeling pleased with the way her new life was panning out.

But she felt miserable.

In some ways, Colt's betrayal hurt even more than finding out about her husband's cheating. She knew it was because of the special connection she shared with Colt. When they'd been out riding trail on Thunder Ranch, she'd truly believed that it would be impossible to find another man more perfect for her than he was.

Everything she loved about Montana and ranching, he loved, too. But their connection went deeper than that. She craved everything about him: his touch, his smile, his voice.

How was she supposed to live without all of those things?

How was she supposed to go on without him?

When the door to the office opened, she looked up, expecting to see Sarah. Leah had delivered her invoice to the house that morning and Sarah had agreed to bring her a check around noon. Maybe she'd decided to drop by earlier.

But it wasn't Sarah.

Colt stood at the door, in the same clothes he'd worn on the weekend, with one addition. His shirt was unbuttoned and bandages swaddled his chest.

"What happened to you?" She was out of her chair and moving toward him, before she could think about how angry she was at him. She stopped a few feet away, suddenly remembering all that stood between them.

Her question could have applied to so many things. How had he been injured? Was he okay? Why hadn't he come home as planned last night?

But Colt chose to answer another question first.

"That woman you saw? That was Janet Greenway. Evan's mother."

It took Leah a moment to process his words. "The pretty blonde—she's the woman who had your baby?"

Colt nodded. "Can we talk?"

"Of course."

He shut the door behind himself. He looked nervous…and, despite his injuries, so damn handsome. Why did this man always have such an effect on her?

"I've been working hard to get my life straightened

up, Leah. You know I talked to Mom about handling more responsibility here at the ranch. But, even more importantly, I needed to sort out my relationship with my son, and in order to do that, I needed Janet's okay."

"And what did she say?" Leah hadn't forgotten about his injury. She meant to get the whole story about what happened. But he must be okay if he was standing here. And this—his son—was more urgent. Obviously Colt had a lot to tell her.

"Janet said yes. But she warned me not to hurt him. I think that's when she hugged me. I saw you and the kids, but I didn't realize you'd seen me, too. And I was so preoccupied with my own nervousness and excitement about meeting Evan for the first time—it never occurred to me that you might misinterpret my conversation with Janet. That you might see it in any sort of romantic context."

"Oh, my Lord." Leah realized she was trembling. She'd been wrong about Colt. The relief was almost overwhelming.

"I did meet Evan, by the way," Colt continued. "And he's a really neat kid. He's into baseball, but he seemed impressed when I showed him Midnight. I'm going to watch one of his baseball games next week. Janet's sending me the schedule."

Leah smiled. "You sound excited."

"It was really great. I had no idea I'd feel that way. He looks so much like me at that age."

"I'm happy for you, Colt. And proud, too. I know it took courage to take that step."

"It's thanks to you that I did it. You made me see what was right. You've made me see a lot of other things, too."

He moved closer to her, but when she automatically stepped back, lines of worry creased his forehead.

"What's going on, Leah? You moved out of my trailer...."

She looked down at her hands, which she had clasped in front of her. "I guess I jumped to the wrong conclusion, when I saw you and Janet together. Maybe I overreacted. But it still makes me wonder how things would work long-term with us. If there's no underlying trust, our relationship is doomed to fail."

"But you *can* trust me, Leah. I love you."

She closed her eyes, relishing the sound of those words. But did he truly mean them? He'd been a wandering cowboy for so long. Could she really believe that the changes he was making were real and permanent?

He stepped forward again, and this time she didn't back away. She touched his bandages gently. "Does it hurt a lot?"

"Cracked rib." He shrugged. "Doesn't hurt as much as the thought that you might not love me back. I know I'm not a great catch. And maybe I don't seem like a good risk, either. But I can tell you right now that you're the only woman I've ever said 'I love you' to. Maybe you don't feel the same about me. If so, just tell me."

He faced her like a man expecting a blow. And Leah's defenses crumbled. "I *do* love you, Colt. But how can I have faith that your love won't change? There are going to be times when we can't be together and I'm going to have to trust you. I'm just not sure that I'll be able to do that."

"When we're apart, just picture me beside you, because that's where I'll always rather be." He stroked the side of her face, gently tucked her hair behind her ear. "Remember when we took that trail ride together?"

Her lips curved into a small smile. "I was just thinking about that day."

"It was pretty wonderful, wasn't it? Our life could be like that day—one long trail ride together."

"That's so poetic."

"You bring it out in me." He ran his fingers under her chin and lifted her face so he could kiss her. His lips brushed against hers temptingly. Soon they were kissing deeply, only stopping when Colt drew her in closer, then immediately groaned.

"I'm sorry." She pulled back from his chest. "I hurt you."

"No. The only thing that will hurt is if you turn me down."

She tilted her head. "What do you mean by that?"

"I'm asking you to marry me, Leah. Let me be the man at your side for the rest of your life."

Leah's heart soared. And at that moment she knew she wanted nothing more, that if she was to live her life fully she had to trust these feelings and trust this man.

"You know Jill, Davey and I come as a package deal."

"I am *so* good with that. But I'm a package deal, too. I come with a big, crazy family, and this ranch, and my son, Evan—he's part of the deal, too. Not sure how big a role I'll get to play in his life, but whatever he needs, I want to be there for him."

She cupped his face in her hands and stared into his eyes. "Tell me this is really happening."

"I can't. You still haven't given me an answer."

She laughed. It was true. This hunk of a rodeo star, this man who felt like her best friend, her soul mate and the sexiest cowboy she'd ever seen, really was hers for keeps.

"Yes, Colton Hart, I will marry you. Let's make it soon, okay?"

"All right!" He threw his hat in the air, then grabbed her again. This time there were no moans of pain as he crushed her to his chest. Only happiness.

Epilogue

One week later

"But why do you have to elope?" Prue Stockton had slowly come around to the idea of her daughter marrying again. Leah was grateful for her mother's acceptance and Colt's patience. He'd worked hard to win her over. He'd been to dinner three times this week, fixed a few things around the house for her mom and spent a lot of hours talking with her on the back patio.

Finally he'd convinced her that he truly did love Leah and that he planned to care and provide for her children like they were his own.

"I've done the big wedding thing before," Leah replied. "I don't feel the need for a huge party. Plus Colt's family just had a big celebration for Ace and Flynn. We'd rather focus on the two of us. Does that seem selfish?"

"No. I do understand. But there is one thing I must insist that you do, and that's phone Jackson and tell him the news. He's still your children's father and he deserves to hear about this from you."

Knowing she was right, Leah had bitten the bullet and called her ex that evening.

"God, Leah, it's only been a year."

"And I suppose you've been celibate since we separated?"

"No, but marriage? That's serious."

"Believe me, I appreciate that. And I also realize this must seem sudden to you, but I've known Colt almost my whole life. We were only friends before. But somehow, when we met up again this time, everything clicked for us."

"What about Jill and Davey? How are they taking this?"

"They like Colt and he's good with them. But you're their father. They love you, Jackson, and that won't change. As long as you make time for them in your life, I'll do everything I can to keep your bond with them strong."

Jackson was silent for a bit. Then he said, "I appreciate that."

"Jill and Davey's happiness is the most important thing to me."

"Me, too. Thanks for calling. Maybe I'll come out to Montana in July and take the kids for a little camping holiday."

"They'd love that."

The conversation ended then, and though Jackson hadn't extended his good wishes to her and Colt, Leah was pleased. For the first time since the divorce, Jackson had expressed a genuine interest in spending time with his children. It was more than she had dared hope for.

THE NEXT MORNING Colt and Leah left to get married. Prue had happily agreed to take the children for two days, with plans for their babysitter, Jessica, to spell her for four hours in the afternoons.

The luxury of two days without children was something Leah hadn't experienced since she'd given birth to Jill. Now she was thrilled to spend those days with Colt.

They drove to Great Falls, where they caught a flight to Vegas. What happened in Vegas was *definitely not* going to stay in Vegas where she and Colt were concerned. As they placed rings on each other's fingers, she said to him, "This is forever, cowboy."

"Damn right it is. I love you, Leah."

They'd kissed, and gone straight to their hotel room. And that was where they stayed until it was time to catch a cab to the airport—with a brief stop at an outlet mall to buy gifts, before catching their plane.

LEAH AND COLT arrived home to Thunder Ranch fifteen minutes before the scheduled Sunday family dinner. Leah had promised Sarah that they would be on time, but she could tell the family was pleasantly surprised when they joined them on the patio, where everyone was gathered for a drink and appetizers.

The day had been hot and most of the women were wearing sundresses, the men jeans and T-shirts. Leah had on a violet-colored, sleeveless shift and strappy sandals that she'd bought on a whim at the outlet mall.

She figured the money was worth it, since Colt couldn't seem to keep his eyes or his hands off her. Though, truthfully, that had been the case before she bought the new outfit, as well.

She had new toys for the children and boxes of specialty tea for Sarah and Prue. But she wasn't pulling those out now.

"Hey, look who's here. And early, even." Dinah was the first to spot them. She was sitting at the edge of the pool, dangling her bare legs in the water. She clambered up and went to hug Leah. "You must be a good influence on him."

Then she hugged Colt. "Well, aren't you the one for surprises. I felt like kicking you when Mom told me about Evan. But marrying Leah was a smart move." She kissed his cheek. "Be happy, okay?"

Jill and Davey had been swimming in the pool with Ace and they were up next, running at Leah and hugging her—almost as tightly as she hugged them back. She couldn't care less that they were sopping wet.

"Oh, I missed my peanuts." Leah kissed each soft cheek about five times. "Were you good for your grandma?"

Prue Stockton was sitting in the shade of the umbrella at the patio table with Sarah and Joshua. Her smile was warm and genuine. "They were themselves, which is exactly the way I love them. We had a lot of fun. And you were only gone for two days, honey. You could have taken a longer holiday...."

Leah went to kiss her mother next. "Thank you. But this is the place we most want to be. With all of you." Then she kissed Sarah, who took her hand and gave it a squeeze.

"I'm so happy, dear. You look lovely. And I've never seen Colt so happy and contented."

It was true. Colt had a new inner peace about him. And with it came a strength that Leah knew she would be able to count on during the tough times. Just as she would be strong for him when he needed her.

Cousins Duke and Beau came to congratulate them next. Duke apologized that he still had no leads on the theft. In fact, there'd been more bad news as another local ranch had been broken into that week.

"We will get to the bottom of it," Duke vowed.

Dinah nodded. "Yes, we definitely will."

Ace came out of the pool then, and Flynn tossed him a towel. He ignored it, and gave her a big hug, which made her laugh, even as she chided him for getting her wet. He went to his brother next.

"So it's official."

Colt brandished his new wedding band proudly.

"Couldn't be happier for you." Ace hugged Colt, then Leah, before turning to Jill and Davey, who were trying to get Zorro to play fetch with them.

"Hey, Jill," Ace called, "what do you think about your mommy eloping with my brother?"

"Ace," his mother scolded, "Jill doesn't know what that word means."

"Yes, I do," Jill insisted, wet braids flopping vigorously as she nodded. "It means Davey and I get a number-two daddy. But our number-one daddy is the one in Calgary and he'll always be our number-one daddy."

Leah's heart swelled with love. "You got that right, peanut." She turned to Colt and she could tell that he was thinking of Evan. She draped her hands around his neck and rested her head on his shoulder.

"He'll be at the Hart family dinners, too, one day," she predicted.

Colt held on to her tightly. "I hope so."

"Believe it. You're going to make a terrific dad." She planted a kiss on his cheek. "Not to mention husband."

Colt shook his head with wonder. "Never thought I'd see the day where I could say that I had it all. I used to be so envious of Ace. Now, I'm just happy for him."

"Look at your mom's smile. She seems pretty happy, too."

"Why not? Two sons married and settled down and a

whole batch of grandkids to go with them. But I know she won't truly be happy until Tuf comes home."

"And how about you?"

"I miss my younger brother. But I have faith in him. Wherever he is, he's doing what he thinks is right. But when he finally does come home—boy, have I got a lot to tell him!"

* * * * *

Be sure to come back to Thunder Ranch and find out who lassos the next cowboy in the Hart family in DUKE: DEPUTY COWBOY by Roz Denny Fox. Available in September 2012 wherever Harlequin books are sold.

COMING NEXT MONTH from Harlequin®
American Romance®
AVAILABLE SEPTEMBER 4, 2012

#1417 DUKE: DEPUTY COWBOY
Harts of the Rodeo
Roz Denny Fox
Duke Adams is a solid, dependable lawman, great with kids and a champion bull rider. He'd be perfect—except Angie Barrington can't stand rodeo cowboys....

#1418 THE COWBOY SOLDIER'S SONS
Callahan Cowboys
Tina Leonard
Retired from military service, Shaman Phillips comes to Tempest, New Mexico, to find peace. The last thing he expects to find is a blonde bombshell who just might be the key to his redemption.

#1419 RESCUED BY A RANGER
Hill Country Heroes
Tanya Michaels
Hiding out in the Texas Hill Country, single mother Alex Hunt is living a lie. But can she keep her secrets from the irresistible lawman next door?

#1420 THE M.D.'S SECRET DAUGHTER
Safe Harbor Medical
Jacqueline Diamond
Eight years ago, after Dr. Zack Sargent betrayed her trust, Jan Garcia broke their engagement and moved away...never telling him she kept the child she was supposed to give up for adoption.

You can find more information on upcoming Harlequin®
titles, free excerpts and more at www.Harlequin.com.

HARCNM0812

REQUEST YOUR FREE BOOKS!

2 FREE NOVELS PLUS 2 FREE GIFTS!

 Harlequin®

 American ★ Romance®

LOVE, HOME & HAPPINESS

YES! Please send me 2 FREE Harlequin® American Romance® novels and my 2 FREE gifts (gifts are worth about $10). After receiving them, if I don't wish to receive any more books, I can return the shipping statement marked "cancel." If I don't cancel, I will receive 4 brand-new novels every month and be billed just $4.49 per book in the U.S. or $5.24 per book in Canada. That's a saving of at least 14% off the cover price! It's quite a bargain! Shipping and handling is just 50¢ per book in the U.S. and 75¢ per book in Canada.* I understand that accepting the 2 free books and gifts places me under no obligation to buy anything. I can always return a shipment and cancel at any time. Even if I never buy another book, the two free books and gifts are mine to keep forever.

154/354 HDN FEP2

Name _____ (PLEASE PRINT)

Address _____ Apt. #

City _____ State/Prov. _____ Zip/Postal Code

Signature (if under 18, a parent or guardian must sign)

Mail to the **Reader Service:**
IN U.S.A.: P.O. Box 1867, Buffalo, NY 14240-1867
IN CANADA: P.O. Box 609, Fort Erie, Ontario L2A 5X3

Not valid for current subscribers to Harlequin American Romance books.

Want to try two free books from another line?
Call 1-800-873-8635 or visit www.ReaderService.com.

* Terms and prices subject to change without notice. Prices do not include applicable taxes. Sales tax applicable in N.Y. Canadian residents will be charged applicable taxes. Offer not valid in Quebec. This offer is limited to one order per household. All orders subject to credit approval. Credit or debit balances in a customer's account(s) may be offset by any other outstanding balance owed by or to the customer. Please allow 4 to 6 weeks for delivery. Offer available while quantities last.

Your Privacy—The Reader Service is committed to protecting your privacy. Our Privacy Policy is available online at www.ReaderService.com or upon request from the Reader Service.

We make a portion of our mailing list available to reputable third parties that offer products we believe may interest you. If you prefer that we not exchange your name with third parties, or if you wish to clarify or modify your communication preferences, please visit us at www.ReaderService.com/consumerchoice or write to us at Reader Service Preference Service, P.O. Box 9062, Buffalo, NY 14269. Include your complete name and address.

Welcome to the Texas Hill Country! In the third book in Tanya Michaels's series HILL COUNTRY HEROES, *a desperate mother is in hiding with her little girl. The last thing she needs is her nosy Texas Ranger neighbor getting friendly....*

Alex raised her gaze, starting to say something, but then she froze like a possum in oncoming headlights.

"Mrs. Hunt? Everything okay?"

She eyed the encircled silver star pinned to his denim button-down shirt. He'd been working this morning and hadn't bothered to remove the badge. "Interesting symbol," she said slowly.

"Represents the Texas Rangers."

"L-like the baseball team?"

"No, ma'am. Like the law enforcement agency." Maybe that would make her feel safer about her temporary new surroundings. He jerked his thumb toward his house. "You have a bona fide lawman living right next door."

Beneath the freckles, her face went whiter than his hat. "Really? That's…" She gave herself a quick shake. "Come on, Belle. Inside now. Before, um, before that mud stains."

"Okay." Belle hung her head but rallied long enough to add, "Bye-bye, Mister Zane. I hope I get to pet Dolly again soon."

From Alex's behavior, Zane had a suspicion they wouldn't be getting together for neighborly potluck dinners anytime in the near future. Instead of commenting on the kid's likelihood of seeing Dolly again, he waved. "Bye, Belle. Stay fabulous."

She beamed. "I will!"

Then mother and daughter disappeared into the house, the front door banging shut behind them.

"Is there something about me," he asked Dolly, "that makes females want to slam doors?"

The only response he got from the dog was an impatient tug on her leash. "Right. I promised you a walk." They started again down the sidewalk, but he found himself periodically glancing over his shoulder and pondering his new neighbors. Cute kid, but she seemed like a handful. And Alex Hunt, once she'd calmed from her mama-bear fury, was perhaps the most skittish woman he'd ever met. If she were a horse, she'd have to wear blinders to keep from jumping at her own shadow. Zane wondered if there was a Mr. Hunt in the picture.

Be sure to look for RESCUED BY A RANGER
by Tanya Michaels in September 2012 from
Harlequin® American Romance®!

SPECIAL EDITION

Life, Love and Family

NEW YORK TIMES BESTSELLING AUTHOR

KATHLEEN EAGLE

brings readers a story of a cowboy's return home

Ethan Wolf Track is a true cowboy—rugged,
wild and commitment-free. He's returned home to
South Dakota to rebuild his life, and he'll start by
competing in Mustang Sally's Wild Horse Training
Competition…. But TV reporter Bella Primeaux
is on the hunt for a different kind of prize,
and she'll do whatever it takes
to uncover the truth.

THE PRODIGAL COWBOY

Available September 2012 wherever books are sold!

www.Harlequin.com

HSE65691